PENGUIN

MIGHTIER THAN THE LIPSTICK

This collection of short stories is a celebration of contemporary women's writing. From around the globe, the stories reflect some of the ways women are viewed and the way they see themselves. From a mother's anxiety that her daughter is too close to her best friend, a young girl imagining her first love and experiencing a bitter reality, to two Indian girls trying to fight against the injustices in their society; they portray different facets of the world today. Painful, amusing, astute and invigorating, this collection will touch and enchant readers everywhere.

Susan Adler was Gender/Equal Opportunities Librarian for ILEA and compiled the Penguin booklists *Ms Muffet Strikes Back* (non-sexist books) and *Equality Street* (non-racist books).

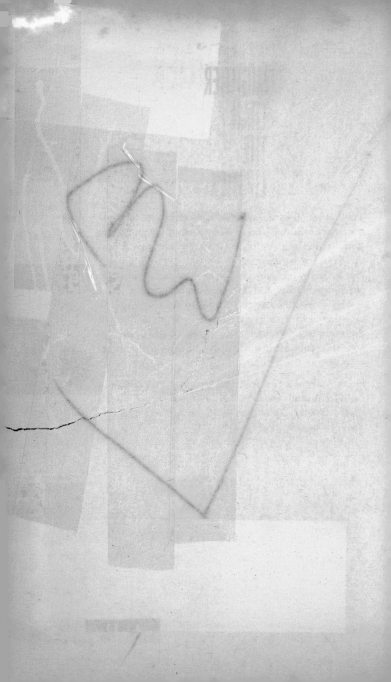

MIGHTIER THAN THE LIPSTICK

Edited by
SUSAN ADLER

PENGUIN BOOKS

For Kathy

PENGUIN BOOKS

Published by the Penguin Group
Penguin Books Ltd, 27 Wrights Lane, London w8 5TZ, England
Penguin Books USA Inc., 375 Hudson Street, New York, New York 10014, USA
Penguin Books Australia Ltd, Ringwood, Victoria, Australia
Penguin Books Canada Ltd, 10 Alcorn Avenue, Toronto, Ontario, Canada M4V 3B2
Penguin Books (NZ) Ltd, 182–190 Wairau Road, Auckland 10, New Zealand

Penguin Books Ltd Registered Offices: Harmondsworth, Middlesex, England

This selection first published by Viking 1990
Published in Penguin Books 1992
1 3 5 7 9 10 8 6 4 2

This selection copyright © Susan Adler, 1990
All rights reserved

Printed in England by Clays Ltd, St Ives plc
Filmset in Linotron Ehrhardt

Contents

Preface

'It should leave you with a pang.' A friend of mine described this as the essential quality of a good short story. That's not to say that reading short stories should be painful but that the best short stories give a feeling of recognition or revelation. All the stories in this collection, whether comic or serious (and most are both), have this ability to startle and disquiet. They are beguiling, memorable and they resonate; their ideas, moods and images return to haunt the reader.

I chose the stories here primarily for the strength of their writing – the power of the pen – and their exceptional portrayal of women and women's lives in the contemporary world. In making the selection, I read and read and read, enjoying stories published in feminist collections and magazines, anthologies of women's writing and more general collections. I was looking mainly for modern fiction about young women and girls and decided to include only stories written by women. Although there is far more literature by and about women published now as compared with the almost all-male cast of the books I read as a teenager, there is still not enough – I'd like to see 51 per cent of the books on the shelves by, and about, women.

Ten of the stories have been published before. How I got the new one 'The Ripening of Time' is itself a story. I was in a crowded café in London, talking with a friend (not the one with the pang-theory – there have been many conversations on the way to this book). I was telling her about the progress and problems of compiling the collection when the woman seated next to us said, 'Excuse me, I couldn't help overhearing . . . I've written a story you may find interesting.' She told me her name and by a strange coincidence I had a copy of a book she had co-edited with me. I felt sure that her story would be right, and when I read it that feeling was confirmed. The moral of this is 'Speak up for yourself' and I hope that reading these stories, some potential women writers may feel inspired to do just that.

My thanks to Helene Fawcett for her ideas and for listening and, of course, to the authors who have contributed to this collection.

Susan Adler
September 1989

Fat Chance

JEAN HOLKNER

My sister Lily is always going on a diet. Or just coming off one.

The last time she made me go on the diet with her.

'Just look at you,' she said. 'If you don't do something soon, people will start mistaking you for Hanny Bergelman.'

This was a pretty cruel thing to say.

Hanny Bergelman was in Lily's form five at the high school and she was the fattest girl in Carlton – maybe even the world. I got up and went to the mirror to see if it was true.

Lily came and stood beside me and we both looked sadly at our reflections. The short fat one was Lily, the tall fat one – me.

'It's all that chicken soup that Mum makes us eat,' said Lily.

'There's a new diet in this month's *Youth and Beauty* magazine,' said Lily and she went to get it.

I knew all about *Youth and Beauty*. It was full of articles with titles like 'How to Disguise a Prominent Nose', 'Living With Your Pimples', and 'Are Your Legs Too Thin?' The last one was useless of course. Nothing about Lily or me had ever been too thin.

'Here it is,' said Lily. 'The Egg and Grapefruit Diet: Lose seven pounds in six days. Six days! That gives me just enough time to be able to squeeze into my red dress for the fifth-form social on Saturday night . . .'

And that's how we came to start on the Egg and Grapefruit Diet.

It was a pretty strict diet. Every meal was the same. Two hard-boiled eggs and one grapefruit and nothing in between except cold water.

'It's just as well Mum's in Hepburn Springs this week,' I said. 'She'd kill us if she knew.'

'By the time she gets back,' said Lily, 'it'll be too late. We'll be slim.'

Maybe it was the novelty of it all but the first day didn't go too badly – till egg number six came up.

I sat and looked at it.

'Come on,' said Lily encouragingly. 'Get it down. Then you'll only have thirty eggs to go.'

So I got it down.

I don't remember much about the second day. Just a yellow and white haze of eggs and grapefruit.

Lily kept getting on the scales every hour or so. But nothing changed. She was still eight stone twelve.

I didn't go anywhere near the scales. After the initial shock of finding that I weighed nearly ten stone I decided to wait till the diet was over and give myself a pleasant surprise at the end. Meanwhile we were getting completely fed up with hard-boiled eggs.

'Why don't we hard-poach them for a change?' I suggested.

So we did, but you could hardly tell the difference.

'Tonight,' said Lily, 'we are going to have an omelette.'

'Omelettes have to have something inside them,' I said. 'Like cheese or fried onions, or both.' And my mouth began to water excitedly.

'We are going to have something inside them,' said Lily. 'Haven't you ever heard of a grapefruit omelette?'

'Count me out,' I said.

That night I watched her as she beat up the eggs, added slices of grapefruit and folded it all over just like a real omelette. 'It's not all that bad,' she said, but I could tell by the look on her face that she was lying and I ate my eggs the normal hard-boiled way.

After tea Lily tried to get into her red dress with the silver roses on the shoulder but she got stuck half-way and I had to haul her out.

'It's too early,' I said. 'You know what they say: for the first two or three days you don't lose anything, and then you suddenly start shedding pounds and pounds.'

'I hope you're right,' said Lily.

'I think we ought to do some exercises as well as diet,' I said. 'Why don't we go to the City Baths and have a swim?'

'Because I can't get into my bathers,' said Lily.

'How about a walk in the park?'

'You go if you like,' she said. 'I'll just stay here and do some exercises on my own – you know – toe-touching and press-ups.'

So I left Lily trying to get into her shorts and I went for a walk by myself.

I'd intended to walk all the way round the cemetery, but, by the time I got there, it was getting dark and I thought I could hear strange noises coming from inside so I decided I'd better go home and help Lily with her press-ups.

'I did seven,' she said as soon as I got inside the door, 'and I hope it was worth it because I think I've put a permanent crick in my neck.'

Luckily her neck was better next morning, but we didn't do any more exercises after that.

On Thursday I decided to stay in bed for a while to make the day a bit shorter. I was lying there thinking about toasted crumpets dripping with honey and French toast sprinkled with sugar, when I suddenly remembered that you had to dip the bread in beaten egg, so I immediately stopped thinking about French toast.

'Breakfast's ready!' called Lily.

I got up and went into the kitchen. She'd mashed up the eggs and grapefruit into a sort of salad and was eating it with her eyes shut.

I sat down and took a mouthful.

'It's no use,' I said, pushing the horrible mess away from me.

'You can't chicken out now,' said Lily.

'Chicken,' I said longingly. 'Chicken and roast potatoes with gravy and baked apples with cream . . . I've had enough,' I said. 'I don't even know why I'm doing it. Our form isn't having a dance next Saturday. Get slim and miserable if you like. I'm staying fat and jolly.' And as I was talking I started taking things out of the pantry – bread, butter, cream, strawberry jam and making myself my favourite sandwich.

From then on we ate separately – Lily with her eggs and grapefruit in the kitchen and me with my triple-decker sandwiches on the dressing-table.

She stopped getting on and off the scales, and instead spent a lot of time doing 'the pinch test'.

The pinch test was designed to help you see how you were going – if you could still grab large handfuls of flesh around your middle it meant you weren't doing too well.

'I must be losing weight,' said Lily. 'There's a lot less in my hand than before . . .'

On Friday morning I was awakened by a loud scream.

I rushed into the bathroom and there was Lily looking down unbelievingly at the scales.

The needle pointed to eight stone seven.

'Five pounds! I've lost five pounds! Where's my red dress?' So we tried again.

This time she got the dress on all right but the zip still wouldn't do up.

'There's still thirty-six hours before the dance,' I said. 'Maybe you should give up eating altogether till then.'

'That's not such a bad idea,' she said. 'I don't feel much like eating anyway.'

'You do look a bit white,' I said, 'and yellow . . .'

Afterwards I went back to the bathroom and got on the scales myself.

I couldn't believe it. All that eating and I hadn't put on a single ounce. Maybe putting on weight was like taking it off. Nothing for a day or two, then pounds and pounds . . . The thought depressed me so much that I went to the pantry and made myself a tomato sauce and cream sandwich.

Lily didn't eat anything at all on Friday – at least not as far as I could see – and she spent most of Saturday lying on the couch wearing a face-mask of white cheese and gherkin. At six o'clock she went into the bedroom to finish getting ready and at ten to eight she came out.

'You look very nice,' I said.

The dress fitted perfectly. The zip was done up, the silver roses sparkled on her shoulder and round her waist, and her cheeks were pink with excitement and some of Mum's rouge.

At eight o'clock she went off and I settled down with something to eat and chapter ten of *Back from the Dead*.

I'd just got to the part where the faceless head appears at the window when I heard the key turn in the front door.

I looked at my watch. It was barely nine o'clock.

Lily came in slowly and sank into the nearest chair.

'What happened?' I said. 'What are you doing home so early?'

She took a deep breath.

'I got as far as the cloakroom,' she said.

'Yes?'

'You wouldn't believe it. Hanny Bergelman was there.'

'So?'

'She was putting on some lipstick.'

'Go on.'

Lily paused. She closed her eyes for a moment. 'She was wearing my dress.'

'What do you mean?'

'I mean she had on exactly the same dress. Can you imagine? It was about four times the size of mine, but it was the same colour with the same silver roses. Everything.' Poor Lily buried her face in her hands.

'What happened?' I asked.

'We stared at one another for a moment, then she walked over and stood right in front of me. Do you realize that besides weighing nineteen stone she's six feet tall? Anyway that's how it felt to me. So she looked down at me and said, "Well, which one of us is going home?"

'The way she said it I knew it had better be me. Anyway by

that time I hated the sight of the dress . . . I'll never wear it
again . . .'

She stopped and looked at the plate beside me.

'What have you got there?' she asked.

'Oh, just some apple pie I found in the freezer . . .'

'Is there any left?'

'Plenty,' I said. 'I'll get you some.'

I got up and went to the door.

'Put loads of cream on it,' she said. 'I'm starving.'

True Romance

JANE ROGERS

First Look

1. *At last, across the crowded room, he managed to catch her eye. She gazed back at him, arrested, beautiful and unselfconscious as a wild creature facing a man; curious, but entirely other. She was lovely, and he knew then he must have her. It was love at first sight.*

2. I really can't remember.

First Kiss

1. *She looked forward to Sunday all week, and time passed so slowly it seemed more like a year. But like all good things, it proved a day well worth waiting for. There was a gusty, fitful wind and brave silvery sunshine, with fleecy little clouds racing across the great bare sky. He was waiting for her at the gate, as he said he would be, and his stern tanned face broke into a wide smile as he saw her battling against the wind towards him. He helped her over the gate and they walked together along the clean-washed beach, leaning forward into the wind, breathless and laughing. There was no need to talk – they were together. He reached for her hand, and she allowed his to brush hers, then teasingly drew it away. He glanced at her, her eyes were sparkling with delight. Light as a leaf in the wind she spun away from him across the sand, her laughter tinkling behind her – and danced down to the sea's edge. He started to move after her, then froze for a moment as his heart lurched to a sudden love for her, as she ran, abandoned as a child,*

towards the sea, her blonde hair streaming out behind her. As he watched she reached the water's edge and stopped, a tiny fearless figure facing the great blue ocean, as if unaware of, or defying, the dangers and terrors those deeps held. He yearned to protect that fearlessness, to guard that innocent trust; to stand with her, to face together that great hazardous sea.

With a sense of passionate urgency he ran towards her, and as he approached she seemed to sense him and she turned to meet him. He grasped her violently in his arms and bent his lips to hers in a kiss that ran through her lips and body like a fire, melting her to him, fusing them together, man and woman, one being, in the promise of love.

2. On Sunday we were supposed to be going for a walk. It was very windy. I didn't want to go, when it came to it; it looked cold, and I was sure we would run out of conversation. We couldn't agree on where to go, I knew the wind would be terrible on the beach, coming straight off the sea, and I wanted to go along the valley which was at least reasonably well sheltered. But he wanted the beach. Which is where we went in the end. I was right, the wind was fierce, the spray spattered on us like rain. He was very jokey and talkative to begin with, talking about a film he'd seen last night (on his own?) and making jokes about English summers. But going along that beach was hard work. You had to keep your head down and your eyes half closed to stop the sand getting in; lean at a forty-five degree angle forwards into the wind; and shout at the top of your voice if you wanted to be heard above the roaring and crashing. I was wearing my anorak and it blew up with air so that I must have looked like a walking Michelin man. I just couldn't think of anything to say. Every now and then I could feel he was looking at me, so I'd look back at him and he'd give a smile or else look away quickly, so in the end I felt awkward and didn't know where to look.

After a bit he started talking, asking me things, I could hardly hear a word and had to keep screaming 'What?' and pointing to my ears to show I couldn't hear. He was asking me about my family and how long we'd lived here. Deliberately thinking of things to keep a conversation going. I wanted to say, if he must talk, why not go up further over the sand dunes so we'd be more protected? But I felt embarrassed to suggest it – couples go in the dunes – and anyway it would have meant we'd *have* to talk. When he gave up for a minute I ran off in front of him, partly to escape the next 'what?', partly because I was beginning to feel such a lump, plodding along. It would look as if I was enjoying it. I was, in a way, but it felt so awkward. I could have cheerfully run on, away, at full speed. He came running after me so I really put a spurt on, but he caught up with me in the end – grabbed my arm and I fell over on the sand. He leant over close to pull me up but instead of letting myself be pulled up I grabbed at his hands and pulled him sideways, so that he stumbled and fell heavily. I got up and stood laughing at him. But I felt awkward. I'd been too violent. I must have seemed like a silly kid – horse play. Was he trying to pull me towards him? I felt completely embarrassed, and started walking on. He caught up with me but didn't say anything. We walked back most of the way in silence. When we got to where the track meets the beach he stopped, poking a shell around with his toe in the sand. Then he picked it up again and said, 'Look.' I went to take it from him and he grabbed my hand. 'What?' I said, feeling foolish. I wished he'd get on with it, I could feel myself going red. He pulled me near and kissed my mouth, then he let go my hand and put his arm round my neck. He was pressing my head to him. He didn't just kiss me, he kept his mouth there, I couldn't breathe. I pushed at his chest and he drew back looking at me in surprise. I laughed, to excuse myself, and ducked under his arm and started to run up the beach. He would think I was stupid, I didn't know what to do. I wanted him to kiss me – I suppose I did – but not – I didn't know what I was supposed to do. Should I have taken my mouth away to breathe then kissed him back? I thought it would look as if I was too eager. I couldn't bear him to know no one had kissed me before.

Every time I thought of it afterwards I went hot with embarrassment; he would think I was a kid.

First Morning

1. He bent over her sleeping head and whispered,

'I love you.' She stirred softly, and reached out her arms. Then she opened her eyes slowly and smiled at him. They embraced again.

'I'm so happy,' she said.

'You look like a fluffy little bird,' he whispered, stroking his hand over her rumpled curls. 'My little nest bird!' Gently, he kissed her lips, her eyes, her cheeks, pulled her tight to him again. 'I could stay here for ever.' She turned her bright head away from him suddenly – 'Look! It's snowed!' He raised his head to look. Excited as a lovely child she jumped out of bed and ran to the window, and clapped her hands.

'It's deep! It's perfectly white everywhere – oh look!'

Rapt, she stared out. He gazed at her profile, pure as a marble statue in the reflected snow light. She turned to him. 'It's for us,' she said. He looked puzzled. 'It's like a new world – everything clean and beautiful, all the dirt and ugliness is covered up, a beautiful white sparkling world – a world for lovers – our new world!' Moved, he got up and went to stand by her. Together they looked out at the dazzling unfamiliar scene.

'We must go out!' she exclaimed. Turning to him, pleading as she saw his expression. 'Just for a little, just to run around and make some footprints. To show we know it's for us!' What a creature of impulse she was! She would be lovely in the snow, but standing here warm beside him, she was even lovelier. He pulled her more closely to him. 'Come back to bed first,' he breathed, in a voice thick with desire. With a mysterious little smile playing at the corners of her mouth, she tilted back her head and surveyed him. She was Cleopatra, mistress of love's secrets, artful. Then as suddenly she was close to him again, surrendered, loving, abandoned in her generosity. He carried her to the bed, watching her precious, familiar ever-new face, entranced; she was all women; like a beautifully cut diamond her many magical sides sparkled and complemented each other. This everchanging love could never end. Burying his face in her hair, he said softly.

'I love you. I love you.' Raising his head thoughtfully for a moment,

speaking almost despite himself, he whispered to the white snow-lit room, 'It's the real thing.'

2. It didn't seem as if I'd slept but I must have done because I opened my eyes and it was very light in the room – it was white. The light seemed unnatural, glaring. My eyes were watering like an old woman's. I turned my head and I could see his shoulder and hair. Carefully, I lifted up the bedclothes and got out of bed. He didn't move. I felt as if I would crack when I moved my legs apart. Very quietly I opened the door and went to the bathroom. The first thing I did was look in the mirror. I half expected – I don't know – to see a different face. At least to see that it had registered somewhere. I expected to look sensual, or experienced, or something. But the same blank face faced me. All its expressions were peeled off and it didn't tell me a thing. It didn't look secretive either. I went to the toilet and then I noticed the blood on my thigh, a thick black smear, dried. My stomach went tight. I started rubbing at it, then I wet some toilet paper and rubbed and scrubbed till it had gone, leaving a red scratched patch on my leg. I filled the sink and washed myself between the legs. It was sore.

When I'd finished I sat on the edge of the bath with the towel around me, I was cold but I didn't want to move. I felt as if I couldn't do anything. I wanted a mother or someone like that to take charge. What happens next? What when he wakes up? I wanted to be alone. I couldn't bear him to look at me till I knew what I was. I was like someone who's had an accident; they don't feel anything for a while, they're numb. I tried to think about it. But I felt nothing. I told myself, 'You've done it at last, you're like everyone else now. The barrier's down.' I tried to laugh at that, but my stone face refused to move. I didn't want to think over the details of it. 'You were glad when it was finished,' I told myself. That must be wrong. I didn't like it. It seemed like nothing.

I remembered I'd read about a custom in a tribe somewhere – in Africa, I expect. Just before a girl is married they keep her away from all the men, in a hut with her mother and all women relatives, and they prepare her. The night before the wedding they have a great feast and dance, with masks and music, a great ritual, the bride dances among the women and the music gets more and more frenzied, beating and beating, and at the climax the headman – with them all watching – he does it to her with a stick, a special kind of stick. And they all sing and celebrate when he shows the blood. They all rejoice. Then her women take her back and clean her and help her, and she meets her husband the next day, without that awful virginity between them. When I read it, it revolted me. Now I wish it had happened to me. Now I wish it had happened to me. It wouldn't be like nothing then; it would really be something.

I noticed the whitish light again and knelt on the toilet seat and lifted up the mucky net curtain to look out. It had snowed – everywhere was covered in white. I started to cry. It was utterly still out there, everything buried under thick snow, and the sky seemed low, deep grey; nothing moved. The whole world had changed in the night. I didn't want to be alone there. I thought we would be together. I did feel pleased in a way, that I'd done it – just because I had, like smoking your first cigarette. But it should be more than that. I was ashamed of my thought, because it made me even more separate from him. The tears kept rolling down my cheeks. I could keep them going, it was soothing. I stopped suddenly. I could see myself. *Wanting* to feel sad. I wasn't sad. I didn't feel anything.

I stay very still now, kneeling, looking out. My head is empty, I stare at the white snow and think nothing and feel nothing except the stillness.

I stare at it till my eyes are full of whiteness, my head is full of whiteness like a million empty pages; it doesn't matter, it hasn't even happened. Nobody knows it's happened except me, maybe it didn't even happen. What would make it real? Nobody knows, it's nothing. Nothing can matter; nothing matters to me. I am snow.

But I imagine him. The ice cracks. I see what he might see. Wondering where I am, coming quietly to the door and listening, then pushing it open slightly. Seeing me kneeling there with the towel round me looking out at the snow. I can see the picture he would see, the narrow brown shoulders and slipping towel and pink feet sticking out soles upwards. The separate captive creature staring out. His heart would melt. He'd come and put his arms around me. He would love my singleness. Yes!

I am posing.

When I went back to the bedroom I was nearly blue with cold but I felt fairly controlled. It was as if I'd put a great distance or age between myself and it. But he was still asleep! I could hardly believe that, it seemed to deny that I existed. I got dressed.

As I was putting my shoes on he woke up. 'Are you up already?'

'Yes.'

'Oh.' I stood for a moment waiting as if my feet were touching a crack in the ice. Say 'Come here', say 'I love you', say 'Are you all right?' He didn't say anything. I went to the window quickly, but my face was burning, because he watched me walk.

'It's snowed.'

'Has it?'

'Yes.' Silence. Suddenly he sat up violently and said:

'I'm starving, it always makes me hungry. Let's go and buy some stuff to cook a big breakfast. Pass my jeans – on that chair.'

I couldn't believe it. 'It always makes me hungry.' While he got dressed I kept looking out the window. But he didn't even notice. He went to the door. 'Are you coming?' He started to go downstairs. He was behaving as if nothing had happened. Well? Nothing had happened.

But I felt frightened, as if I'd thrown something away without knowing its value. I remembered that he'd never even said 'I love you'. I'd been cheated.

In Montreal

KATE PULLINGER

In Montreal Christine was foreign for the first time. She had never been outside the enormous and empty western province in which she had grown up. In fact, she had hardly been away from the small, mountain town where her family lived. To Christine, Montreal seemed as romantic and distant as Paris. Ever since she was a small girl and had seen Quebec on the television, watched those gritty politicians with their gravelly voices and thick accents, she had wanted to go and live there. So, when she was seventeen she packed her bags and, with the money she had made car-hopping in the summer at the Drive-In Restaurant, she boarded an aeroplane and began her adult life.

In Montreal Christine could not speak the language. When she arrived in the terminal and asked for directions to the city in her high school French, she knew immediately that she was out of her depth. The woman at the information desk replied to her in English. But that did not stop Christine. She was brave, determined and stubborn, as only seventeen-year-old girls can be.

Christine knew exactly what she was going to do with her new life in Montreal. She had told her parents she was going to get a job, save some money and then go to university, but she had no intention of doing anything as mundane as that. Christine was going to speak French, dress in black, smoke Gauloises, live by herself, and, best of all, become a lapsed Catholic. In the small town where she had grown up most people were either Presbyterians or members of the United Church, a distinctly Canadian mixture of protestant religions that resembled a sort of extremely low Anglican. Christine was bored with that now. She wanted a religion with some dignity and mystery so that when she rejected it, as she knew she would, she'd have the pleasure of rejecting something particularly rich.

Within a week of her arrival Christine had a job wiping tables and clearing dishes in a café in the bottom of Les Terraces, a shopping complex on St Catherine Street in downtown Montreal. It was one of those totally plastic little places that Montreal enterprise is so bad at, a sub-American kind of dive, decorated in orange and lime-green with mushroom-like tables sprouting out of the concrete floor and dingy mirrors on the walls. Les Terraces, like much of downtown Montreal, is indoors and underground. At Le Hamburger the ventilation worked against the heating and the result was a very hot hamburger bar with grease hanging in the air. But, to Christine, the most extraordinary thing about Le Hamburger was that, despite all appearances, everything about it was absolutely Québécois. *'Un hamburger, s'il vous plaît.'*

Along with the job, which paid much less than the legal minimum wage, a fact she didn't have enough French to complain about, Christine found somewhere to live. From an advert in the window of a small corner tabac she rented a one-room apartment at the top of four flights of stairs down by the river in East Montreal. The windows were cracked and the small radiator hissed and sighed while it pumped out heat. The hot-plate in the corner was coated with grime, and the mattress was lumpy. The obligatory bare light bulb hung from the ceiling in the middle of the room. Christine loved it, of course. It was all hers.

Montreal was all hers as well – Christine felt this as she strolled along the city's streets. The churches, the parks, the cafés, the bar-restaurants that stay open all night, even the taverns on the corners that still did not allow women through their doors; in those first months she often felt like embracing it all. But Montreal was much slower to accept Christine. More often than not when she greeted its inhabitants with her very bad but enthusiastic French she would be answered in English or not at all. The Canadian Language War was at its height and Christine frequently became an unwitting casualty of the hostilities. But youth, determination and zeal protected her as she calmly got on with her life.

During the daytime, from 7.00 a.m. to 5.00 p.m., Christine cleaned up after the boys who hung out at Le Hamburger. While they dealt acid and punched each other on the forearms, she picked up coffee cups and wiped ketchup off the tables. She listened to their raucous conversation, catching the odd word in English: 'car', 'bar', 'pizza', 'acid' and 'hashish'.

From the big bookstore further down St Catherine Street Christine bought herself a book called *How to Speak French* and in the evenings once home from work she read it diligently, practising out loud in front of the mirror. *'Bonjour, madame. Bonjour, mademoiselle. Comment ça va?'* she'd say to herself. *'Ça va bien, et vous? Voulez-vous un hamburger? Non, merci. Je suis fatiguée.'*

On Sundays, her one day away from Le Hamburger, Christine went to mass. She was making a tour of all the Catholic churches in Montreal. This project would take her years to complete, but Christine was undaunted by this in the same way that she was undaunted by much about her new life. She started off with the big ones and on her first Catholic Sunday went to Notre-Dame in Vieux Montreal. Its old world splendour pleased her; the stained glass and high arched ceilings made her feel something she imagined might be akin to Faith.

On the second Sunday Christine attended mass in St Joseph's Oratory, one of the biggest Catholic churches in North America. It sits up on the north-east side of Mont Royale, together with the huge, electrically lit cross that stands further up the mountain. Christine climbed the hundreds of steps that lead up to the church, steps she would later learn to her blatantly protestant distate that thousands of pilgrims had climbed, and were still climbing, on their knees every year. Inside the Oratory, Christine was impressed by the grandeur of the building and the extreme religiosity of the ceremony. She lit a candle and then fell asleep during the service. The mystery of Catholicism was a complete enigma to Christine and besides, it was all in French.

Back at Le Hamburger on Monday morning, Christine communicated with her boss, a small and dark Québécois man named Rene, by smiling, nodding and then going back to work without the slightest idea what he had been saying. He, however, seemed pleased enough with her and Christine believed that he must not realize she could not speak French but merely thought she was a bit quiet. When the boys who hung out directed their conversation towards her, she merely smiled and occasionally said 'Oui'. She had learned by that time how to say 'Oui' with the appropriate Montreal accent rendering it completely unlike anything she had learned in high school. The boys were not convinced.

As spring gradually moved into summer the overheating at Les Terraces became over-air-conditioning. Christine continued to work at the hamburger bar and incorporated into her Sunday tour of the churches lengthy diversions into the Parc Mont Royale where she would spend the afternoon lying in the sun reading French grammar books. She was progressing well with the language, warming up to it with the weather. By June she had learned enough to ask for more money from her boss at Le Hamburger.

One day, a boy who hung out, leaning his thin frame against the orange plastic table for most of the afternoon, drinking cups of Rene's foul coffee and, occasionally, dribbling ketchup over the limp fries that were the speciality of the place, looked up at Christine while she was wiping away spilt sugar from the next table.

'Hello,' he said, in strongly accented English. 'Where are you from?'

'Quoi?' replied Christine.

'Come on,' he said, 'I know you are not French. I know you are an Anglo. Speak up, eh? Where are you from?'

Christine smiled at him. *'Mais, je suis Française.'*

The boy laughed and said, 'You are about as French as Rene's hamburgers.' Christine continued to wipe tables while all around her the boys, No. 7s dangling from their mouths, laughed.

By August, the hottest and stickiest month in Montreal, Christine was reading novels in French and beginning to build up a small collection of books in her room. She was reading Colette and Marie-Claire Blais and had even embarked upon *À la recherche du temps perdu*. During the evening, after she finished work, Christine would leave the cold underground environment of Les Terraces and walk down St Catherine Street, heading east. When she reached St Denis she would turn to the right and find a seat in one of the many cafés that spill out on to the sidewalk. There she would sit sipping a beer and read, ignoring the sweat that ran in rivulets down her back. Usually some jazz would be wafting out of the café and Christine would feel, as the verbs, nouns and adjectives came off the page and told her stories, that she was beginning to understand her adopted language. She would sit and read Proust very happily for several hours until she felt her eyes grow heavy, then, just as the cafés were beginning to fill up with Montrealers out for the evening, she would pick up her book, empty her glass of beer, and walk home to her little room.

At about ten o'clock one evening, the time Christine usually headed off, a young woman with dark eyes and a mass of curly hair stopped beside her table. '*Bonjour*,' she said, and still speaking in French, 'Is anyone sitting here?'

'No,' said Christine, in French, 'please sit down. I was just about to leave.'

'Oh,' said the woman, 'you are not French?'

'No,' said Christine, 'I come from the West.'

'But you speak French? Where do you live, here, in Montreal?'

'Yes, I live down by the river.'

'By yourself?'

'Yes.'

'But that is very brave,' replied the woman, who then intro-
duced herself. Marie-Sylvie was a student at the university
nearby. She came from a small town up the St Lawrence River
and did not speak one word of English. Christine talked to her in
French without pausing to think as she did so. They ordered
several beers together and watched while the activity on St
Denis grew more frenetic as the night drew on.

'So,' said Marie-Sylvie. 'You live all by yourself in a tiny room
by the river and you work every day in a greasy café wiping up
after obnoxious boys who treat you badly. You are paid very
little. On Sundays you go to church, although you are not
Catholic and the rest of the time you spend reading French
grammar books. Why?'

'Well,' replied Christine in her young and steady voice. 'It
seemed the only way to begin to learn how to think in French.'

Around midnight Christine got up to leave. It was still very hot
and when she stood she suddenly felt quite drunk.

'*Au revoir*. Will we meet again?' she asked Marie-Sylvie whose
dark hair was damp with sweat.

'*Au revoir*,' said Marie-Sylvie, 'I come here often; I am sure
we will.'

Christine wove her way through the tables of the café and
began to walk back down St Denis towards St Catherine Street.

War of the Worlds

RAVINDER RANDHAWA

'You two want to do what you want? Behave as you please?' Mum's voice hard and strained, refusing to shed the tears flooding her eyes. 'If you don't like living here, you can leave. Both of you.' It was like being given ECT. Little shockwaves burned through us. I could see Suki's eyes growing larger and larger, expanding exponentially. Mum had never said anything like this to us before.

She'd never blamed us before, she'd blamed the nurse in the hospital when we were born. 'Twin daughters,' she'd told Mum, bearing one on each arm. 'Aren't they sweet? Sweet on the outside, acid on the inside,' she'd said sing-song. 'Oh, they're going to be terrible. The Terrible Twins!' chuckling away.

'Because your father isn't around any more . . .' Mum still couldn't bring herself to use words like dead . . . 'you think you no longer need to watch your tongue, or have respect for other people. And you never have to come back. Have your freedom.' Scooping up the baby, marching off upstairs.

It wasn't that we'd changed, things had. We'd been wilder than wild even when Dad was alive: running round town like we were urban guerrillas of the Asian kind. No part of town we didn't know, no person we didn't sus out, no action we didn't know about. The town was our battleground. Our Frontline. Dad would rave and rant at us, tell us we were shameless, not fit to live in civilized society and did we know what happened to women like us? Dad wanted us to be accommodating, to fit in, to live like decent people. We know what 'decent' people get up to when they think no one's looking, we argued back, like there seems to be one set of rules people use if they think they're going to be found out and another set if they think they can do whatever they want in safe secrecy. And it's not as if everyone doesn't know what's going on. They're all happy to shut their eyes to it 'cos they don't want to rock the boat and they don't want to grass on anyone else in case they get grassed on themselves.

Mum and Dad copped it from us every time. We were part of them and they were part of us and that's why we could never be soft with them. If we got them to agree with us, just once, it was like the gates were opened for us to take on the whole world.

And now Mum was saying we could leave. Go. Do what we want. Walk out the front door. We both swivelled our heads to look towards it, though of course we couldn't see it from where we were sitting. Suki and I didn't look at each other; we didn't have to. Mum's ultimatum was ticking like a time-bomb in our brains.

Freedom!

We both stood up, went towards the front door and opened it. It was a beautiful summer evening: balmy, cool, fragrant. Real tourist brochure stuff. We stepped out, over the threshold.

'Charlie's having her party tonight,' said Suki.

'Probably be the same old crowd.'

'We should go to London. Thousands of new people there.'

'Millions. And new things to do.'

'Living on our own.'

'Making it in the Metropolis.'

A car drove by and the bloke in it waved to us. We both waved back, our arms like enthusiastic windscreen wipers. We could hear him reversing his car further up the road, the gravel crunching under his tyres. The blokes loved doing that. Made them feel like Action Man come alive. His engine noise zoomed towards us and then stopped as the car came to a body-shaking, gravel-crunching stop outside our gate.

'You gonna go?' asked Suki.

'I did him last time. He won't know the difference.'

She sauntered off towards him and I sat peeling grass blades, till a pile of curled green strips lay at my feet.

Their voices rose and fell, scraps of sentences floated back to me, followed by occasional riffs of laughter; Suki was leading him on, making him think he had a chance. He didn't of course. He was too ordinary. His flash car and trendy clothes couldn't make up for the mediocre stuff in his brain. I was surprised he hadn't heard of us, hadn't been warned off going near the terrible twins. We had a whole pack of enemies in town, not least among them, the blokes who'd sworn they loved us madly and couldn't live without us. Until we put our reject stamp on them.

Suki and I always compared notes and it was always the same old story: unimaginative, unintelligent. Men who thought they were God's special gift to Asian women. The white blokes wanted to liberate us from our 'primitive' traditions and customs; the Asian blokes thought weren't we lucky to be loved by them in spite of our dubious reputations and bad style of life. Nothing guaranteed to make us run faster and further than blokes imagining themselves to be 'In Love' with us. We'd seen enough of the after-effects of 'In Love' to make us avoid it like the proverbial plague.

First there was Janet, whose bloke had been 'In Love' with her, had chased her for months till she'd finally come round, as they say; come to her senses, he'd said. And Paul had been ever so romantic, insisting on a church wedding, white dress, whisking her off to a grand honeymoon. Janet don't talk about Love no more though – bit difficult when half your teeth been knocked out, and all the other bits of your body knocked in.

Then there was our cousin, Jeeta. Got to be fair, he hadn't said he loved Kulwinder. Just that he forgot to tell her that he'd promised his love to the *gori* next door; just that he didn't have the guts to tell his mother, either, as she busily went about arranging his marriage to Kulwinder. Kulwinder who was sweet, obedient and modest, the perfect Indian girl, the perfect Indian bride.

'Being perfect didn't stop her getting messed up, did it?' said Suki in one of her sarky moods.

Kulwinder did her best. We know she tried hard, but she was too innocent, too simple for his tactics, and he knew she didn't know how to fight back. He wanted to drive her away by driving her to a nervous breakdown; that much she sussed out and flew the nest before the rot could set in.

Suki and I couldn't believe it. The whole family, even our Mum and Dad, sided with him: they said she should have tried harder, been more patient, understanding. Marriage wasn't the easy option the West made it out to be. It had to be worked at, sacrifices and compromises made. 'Sita-Savitri doesn't live here any more, don't you know?' I said. Wasted my inter-cultural mythical allusions, didn't I, 'cos they all turned round and looked as blank as blank at me.

Suki and I wanted to make Halal meat out of Jeeta and serve him up to Kulwinder on a platter, but she wouldn't have none of it. She was too good an Indian girl to get mixed up in revenge and justice, and anyway her father had to think of her future. He'd have to start looking for another marriage for her. She mustn't jeopardize her chances.

Then there was the time we brought Shanti and her baby home.

'They've been thrown out of their home, Mum, and an English woman was trying to help her, but you know how none of these *goras* can speak Punjabi . . .'

'Illiterate lot,' added Suki, interrupting my grand speech. Mum took her in and Mum and Mum's friends all gathered round to help. They brought clothes for Shanti and the baby, they cooked food for them, they condoled, they consoled, they commiserated and then stood back as Shanti and baby went back to her horrible husband. We couldn't understand it and attacked Mum for driving her back.

'Shanti thought it over and made her own choice,' said Mum.

'Some choice,' muttered Suki.

'That's all some women get.'

'It's wrong.'

'Yes,' replied Mum, seeming to agree with us for once, 'but it won't be for long, will it? You two are going to change the world, aren't you?' She could be dead sarcastic, our mum.

We couldn't let it go, could we? We decided on direct action: decided to get them at the Gurudwara. Anyone could get up and speak. The men did it all the time, giving long lectures on righteous living and long-winded explanations of God's thoughts and intentions; they all talked like they had a hot line to the heavens.

We'd made sure we were dressed proper and started off by reading a verse from Suki's *Gotka* (no, she hadn't got religion, just thought it was 'bootiful' poetic stuff. Mum and Dad would get ever so pleased when they saw her reading it – thinking that the light of goodness had finally touched their wayward daughter). I've done a lot of things in my (short) life, but getting up there in front of all them Sunday-come-to-worship-people was the toughest. It started off all sweet and nice, the mothers and grandmothers smiling at us, whispering among themselves about how nice it was to see us young women taking part. I sneaked a glance at Dad. Shouldn't have. His eyes were sending out laser beams of anger. He knew we were up to something.

Finishing the verse, we started in on our talk, speaking our best Punjabi and careful not to let our dupattas slip off our heads. We began by saying that there was much suffering in our community and that we, as the Gurudwara, should organize to do something about it. For instance there should be a fund for women who have to leave home because they are being beaten or ill-treated; the Gurudwara should arrange accommodation as well as helping them with education and training and make sure they weren't outcast by the rest of the community. Rather the Gurudwara should praise them for having the courage to liberate themselves from cruelty, just as India had liberated herself from the cruelty of the Raj (rather a neat touch, I thought: the linking of the personal to the political, the micro to the macro). It was as if the windows had banged open and let in a hot strong wind; a susurration of whispers eddied to and fro.

They didn't know we'd only given them the hors d'oeuvre. We then suggested that the problem should be tackled at the root: men were not going to have respect for women unless they had respect for women's work; therefore the boys should be taught cooking, cleaning, babycare, etc. The men sniggered, some laughed out loud.

'Men who beat or mistreat their wives should be heavily fined by the Gurudwara, and if they persist should be cast out from our society. And if they've taken a dowry they should be made to return it, in double. Blokes who make girls pregnant and then leave them in the lurch should never be allowed to have an arranged marriage . . .' We had to stop 'cos Pati's dad, Harcharan Singh, stood up and launched into an attack on us. We were really disgusted! That man spent more money on his drinking and smoking than he did on his family, and still wanted them to be grateful for whatever scraps he threw their way. This man was now standing up and accusing us of being corrupt and dangerous; others were nodding their heads in agreement.

'Are you saying these things don't happen?' we asked, all innocent like.

I don't think he even heard, just carried on with his diatribe against 'children who don't know their place and women who have no respect for tradition and custom.' Others couldn't wait and interrupted until there were several voices all speaking at once. One voice strained above the others and accused us of bringing dirt and filth into the house of God and getting a bit carried away he let slip a couple of nasty words. Mistake, because Mrs Gill, who was a Moral Majority in her own right, got up immediately and rounded on him like a 40-ton truck. Adjusting her dupatta like a gunslinger adjusting his holster, she told him it was his rotten tongue defiling the house of God and why couldn't the men sit quiet and let the girls finish what they were saying.

'We should listen to our young sometimes,' she said. 'We may learn something.' She gave us the all-clear nod and sat back down among the women.

This was the crunch, the lunge for the jugular vein, and as I formed the words and reached for the microphone I found my voice, Suki's voice, reaching out, spreading across the hall: 'It's no good coming to the Gurudwara once a week to show how clean and pure you are, it doesn't hide all the sordid, underhand things that have been happening all week. The Gurudwara isn't the disinfectant that kills 99 per cent of all germs. It should be treated with more respect. In turn we who are the Gurudwara should get tough on those men who harass us women, whistle at us, touch us up, attempt to force us into their cars . . . Some of them are sitting right here and they know who they are.' Like a storm among the trees angry, aggrieved whispers were rustling around the men . . . 'What about the man who's started a prostitution racket? He's here. And those who can't tell the difference between their daughters and their wives . . .' The place exploded, most rising to their feet, some raising their fists to us, others moving forward, pushing through towards us.

Dad had saved us. Defused the danger. The crowd had parted to let him through.

'I suppose we'll have to call him Moses after this,' whispered Suki. He stopped by us and turned round to face the others.

'It's late. I'm going to take my daughters home. But we can't go without having Prasad.' Picking up the covered bowl of warm Prasad Dad served us each with a round ball of the gorgeous delicious sweet, whispering to us to meet him by the car. He turned round and started serving those nearest to us. Prasad is God's food and you're not supposed to refuse it. You should be glad it's offered to you.

'D-a-d is O-u-r C-h-a-m-p-i-o-n.' All the way home we wanted to chant 'D-a-d is O-u-r C-h-a-m-p-i-o-n', like the football fans do, but he was in a foul mood so we shut up and kept quiet.

'We think what you did was really brave,' said Preeti during the dinner break at school.

'Yeah. Those things really needed to be said,' added Bhupinder, her short pigtails swishing round her face; she never had been able to grow her hair below shoulder length, despite all the creams and lotions she poured on to it.

'So why didn't you say anything?' asked Suki. 'We could have used some help.'

'You kidding? Mum would have come down on me like Two Tons of Bricks.'

'Gutless goons always want other people to do their fighting for them,' I said, hoping it sounded as sarky as I felt.

'No one asked you to do it,' put in Preeti, coming to her best friend's aid. 'Anyway you two fancy yourselves as Revolutionaries.'

'Freedom Fighters,' added stupid Bhupinder with a stupid giggle. 'We wouldn't want to take your glory from you.'

'And not everyone's got liberal parents like yours.' Poison Preeti again.

Liberal parents! That sure was history, what with Mum as good as throwing us out of the house! Suki was trying to say goodbye to the thing at the gate, his arms stretching out to hold her back, impress her with his burning passion. She moved back towards him once, twice, and I thought, this is silly, why's she wasting her time on him when we've got to talk and make decisions?

'You were right. He's a dead loss.' Her skirt swished by me as she sat down.

'There must be some who aren't.'

'We'll have to go looking for them, won't we?'

'Mum doesn't want us here if we don't change.'

'You want to leave?' Suki turned round to look at me, face on, full frontal.

'I'm not scared of leaving.'

'Not the point.'

'There's always white people and white society . . .?' My voice sounded as if posing a maths problem.

'They'll want us to change to their ways . . .' Suki came back as sharp as a knife.

Silence between the two of us. For a change! I picked up the shredded bits of grass and shifted them through my fingers. 'Not much choice, is there? I guess it's a case of Here to Stay-Here to Fight.'

Suki giggled. 'Old slogans never die, eh?'

I had an idea. I thought it was brilliant. 'Let's go to Patel's.' Suki caught on as I knew she would. 'And see if he's got any mangoes for Mum? Right.'

We closed the gate very carefully behind us, in case Mum heard and wondered.

The Healing

DOROTHY NIMMO

We were messing about, which we shouldn't have been doing, but there you are. We should have been outside, but it was freezing out. Karen was showing off doing this flip thing she's just learnt. I don't mind Karen showing off because she's been my friend since the Junior and she's really good, anyway. Then she sort of slipped and she just lay there on the floor.

'Oh Lord,' she said. 'That's torn it!'

And we remembered about the competition.

You might think we were making a big thing about it but there wasn't much you could do around our school that made people think anything of you. Everyone wants to be someone, I mean everyone wants to be special. Don't they? Look at all the people who go on the prize shows on the telly, they'd rather look like prize wallies and be able to say they've been on the telly than spend their whole lives never doing anything.

At our school you do all right if you play football. If you get in the team you do all right. And the big boys have their bikes. They start with the mopeds and then they get the big Hondas, with the fairings and that. They're really big deal on those bikes, with their leathers and boots and their heads twice the proper size in the helmets. You can't see the spots under the visors. And the girls hang round them. There isn't much for the girls. You get noticed if you go around, you know, if you're easy, and if you get pregnant they talk about you but they don't admire you. There isn't much a girl can do apart from swimming and gymnastics.

They put us all in for the competitions, that's the way they

have. They think there's no point in anything unless there's a
competition and a prize. They mean well, they think we're losers
so they'll give us a chance at something, even if it's something
really diddy, like cookery. They had a cookery competition one
time, it was some custard-powder company, they all had to think
up different things you could make with custard powder. Sandra
went in for that because there was a prize, twenty pounds. She
made this cake with custard powder and then custard on top,
you know, and then all different fruit; it was a lovely colour,
really bright yellow, but she didn't win. My Mum does flower
arrangements. Honestly, she spends hours finding this stuff,
dried flowers and leaves, and she has all these different baskets
and bits of log hollowed out. I think it looks terrible. It looks
dead and it stands around the house all winter getting deader
and deader. But she puts these things in the Flower Show and
gets prizes; she gets a real kick out of the prizes. So she says to
me, 'Why don't you make a sponge cake, Marty, there's a class
here for a sponge? Or scones, that's easy, go on. Just for fun. It
doesn't matter if you win or not, that's not the point. It's the
competition is the fun!'

I don't understand her. What's the point of going in for it if
you know you're going to lose? It isn't fun, it's bloody murder, I
think.

Karen used to go in for swimming. She said it was boring
pounding up and down the pool. When they get keen they really
drive you. It must do something for them, I suppose it would, for
the teachers, if they can get a winner out of all of us losers. Karen
was good at the swimming, but then she got something wrong
with her ears and even old Evans thought it was a bit much to go
deaf just so the school could get into the area championships. So
then she took up the gymnastics.

Ever since I've known her she's been doing things like the
crab, going round the playground all bent over backwards, and
cartwheels and that, so she'd got the talent and she really took to
it. Everyone was doing it that year, it was all on the telly and the
girls were really keen, but it was Karen they kept on at to do the

competitions. And there was Karen on the floor. The Championship was the next day.

Someone said she ought to go to the nurse and someone else said, try a hot-water bottle. Sandra said, 'What about an iron?' And we said, 'What do you mean, an iron?'

'You iron her back,' said Sandra, 'I've seen it done.'

'You're having me on,' I said.

'It's the heat,' said Sandra.

'Honestly?' said Pam. Pam believes anything, always has. One time I told her if she put her fingers down her throat she could touch her toes. She believed me. She was sick, you can imagine, all on her shoes.

'What about a rolling pin?' I said, 'we could roll her out.' I didn't think they'd take that seriously.

'I think we ought to go and tell Mr Evans,' said Jenny.

'How are you feeling?' I asked Karen.

'Not bad,' she said. So I knew she felt bad.

'We'd better sort it out for ourselves if we can,' I said.

So then Sandra went and got in at the window of the Home Economics, which is easy for her. I reckon she can get into anything, it's a knack, she says. It'll get her into trouble. She got in at the window and then she got another window open and we all climbed in. Karen said it was easing up a bit, but we made her lie down on one of the tables. First we found the rolling pin and rolled it up and down. You wouldn't think that would do any good; it didn't.

'Roll on a floured board,' said Nell. 'That's what it says in the cookery books!' She thought that was such a good joke she was no help at all for a bit.

'Is that what it means?' said Pam. 'Honestly?'

'Oh Pam!' said Sandra.

Then we got out the iron, Sandra got the cupboard open, and we plugged it in and started ironing Karen's back through her vest until it got too hot and she yelled. And we'd had it on the lowest setting.

Then it was Nell said, 'Let's try the laying-on of hands.'

'Go on,' said Karen, 'what's that?'

'It's what Jesus did, what the healing people do, you know, like in the Bible.'

'I never get in in time for Assembly,' I said.

'We don't have Bible in Assembly any more,' said Pam.

'We always have sex in R.E.' said Jenny.

'But we had it in the Junior,' said Nell, 'Jesus was always at it, putting his hands on people. And they do it up at the Pentecostal. There's a man used to come to the shop ever so lame and now he doesn't.'

'Go on, Karen, let's have a go,' said Sandra.

'Do you have to say anything?'

'Pick up your bed and walk,' suggested Nell.

'I'm not on my bed,' said Karen.

'In the name of the Father and the Son and the Holy Ghost, Amen?'

'I don't know,' said Sandra. 'You go first.'

Nell put her hands on Karen's back and said, 'Get thee behind me, Satan!'

I don't know where she got that from.

Nothing happened. We didn't expect anything to happen, we were just trying it on. Then Pam put her hands on and began stroking and squeezing like the massage people do in the films, but Karen said that made it worse. And then I did it. I put my hands on Karen's back and I could feel the warmth going on down my arm and running into her back. I felt like it was my blood running into her and if I didn't take my hands away I wouldn't have any blood left any more. It was quite hard, taking my hands away. I felt quite weak, honestly.

Karen lay there for a bit. Then she got up.

'How does it feel?' I said.

'It's fine,' she said. 'That's fixed it.'

Then they all started to go on at me.

'What did you do, Mart?' said Sandra.

'I didn't do anything.'

'You must have done something.'

'Try it on me,' said Nell.

'I've got this dirty great spot on my chin,' said Sandra.

'I've got warts,' said Jenny.

But Karen said to leave me alone, we'd better get out before someone caught us.

Karen was third in the competition. Mr Evans said it wasn't good enough.

Sometimes Nell or Sandra get at me about it. If they have a headache or a period pain they say, 'What about a bit of the old laying on of hands, Mart?' But I don't take any notice. They'll forget about it.

I wouldn't like to do it again.

They probably have competitions for that, too. If they knew about it, they'd probably put me in for them. I can just imagine all the sick, lame people laid out on the floor and everyone having a go who can make them get up fastest. With stopwatches and numbers, like they do in competitions. And prizes. I know they don't really. I don't expect I'd win if they did.

Codling-Moth

MARGARET SUTHERLAND

We talk about it a lot. It is as unattainable, as desirable as beauty. In secret we crave it; cynics, we talk about it as we sit together under the gum trees at lunchtime, eating peanut butter sandwiches.

'It's ridiculous, the way they go on about it all the time,' says Mel, tossing her crusts to the predatory gulls. We aren't supposed to feed them but we do. 'I mean, it's one thing in the pictures and books and poetry and that stuff, but take real life. Take my parents. Or yours. They love each other but you don't see them slopping all over each other and going on as though that's all there is to think about. Do you?'

'No, you don't,' I say. When my father comes home he kisses my mother, or rather he kisses the air by my mother's cheek, and if he's late, as he often is when shift work or his mates at the pub delay him, my mother, rattling plates, says, 'Your dinner's in the oven and if you don't hurry up and eat it it'll be dried up to nothing.' I suppose they love each other.

'Of course they have been married a long time,' Mel says, thinking. You know when she is thinking. Her eyes go away from you, like a blind person who, in following the direction of your voice, misses and looks past your shoulder. 'It's probably different when you're married. Romeo and Juliet never got married did they.'

I think of Romeo coming in late from work and Juliet rattling plates and saying, 'Your dinner's in the oven.' It makes me feel sad. Mel and I saw the film. I cried at the end. Mel's more sensible than I am. She doesn't believe in crying, as a rule, but she didn't want to look at me when we came out.

'It's different, being married,' I say, to bring her back to sitting under the trees and feeding the seagulls. 'It must be. I've never seen any married people who love each other so they'd rather die than stay alive if the other one died.'

Mel bites into an apple – glossy, red, perfect. 'Ughff, look at that,' she says, spitting out the words and the apple together, and showing me the core. A dull greyish powder spreads from where the worm has tunnelled.

'Codling-moth,' I say. Mel has a quick look round and shies the apple at the bossiest gull, which lumbers into the air, settles a few feet away, and regards us with the icy outrage of our headmistress objecting to complaints of behaviour on the buses with the boys from St Pat's.

A thought has just occurred to me. 'Maybe they make it up,' I suggest. 'I bet there's no such thing as love. That kind anyway. Maybe people know there isn't and wish there was, so they make it up and write books and compose songs and all the time it isn't true.'

That makes us silent. I wish I hadn't had that thought. I hope I'm wrong.

'I think you're right,' Mel says suddenly. When she's finished thinking, she's back with you, snap; quite startling if you've gone away into your own thoughts while you've been waiting for her. 'There's no such thing. Jolly good thing too. Who wants to go all sloppy and slushy about some idiot with sweaty hands and pimples. It's absolutely disgusting when you think about it. It makes you sick.'

'But they're not all like that,' I say quickly, trying to unthink my thought. 'What about Jolyon Townsend?'

'You certainly see a lot like him,' says Mel, who can be sarcastic. 'At the school ball the floor was littered with boys like him, wasn't it. You tripped over them at every step. Or they tripped over you more likely.'

'Well . . .' I say.

'Well?' she says. Mel likes to be sure she's won the point.

'Well,' I say, 'they can't help it. They might look better when they're older.'

'Like twenty years older.'

'Anyway what about us?' I've remembered the photo of Mel and me, in flocked nylon dance frocks and long mittens, standing in front of the artificial gladioli. 'What about that photo of us?' There is nothing to say.

I try again. 'How about Mr Krassmann then?' I ask in a very insinuating way. I think Mel has a crush on Mr Krassmann, who tutors her privately on Saturday mornings in German. When she came round to my place after her lesson last week her face was quite pink, and *Heute und Abend* isn't the sort of thing to put roses in anybody's cheeks. Mel is giving nothing away.

'Mr Krassmann?' she says, drawing it out as though I've suggested old Harry, the school caretaker, who is about seventy and smells of tobacco. He spits too. 'You must be joking.'

In *The Importance of Being Earnest*, our play for English Lit. this term, Mel has the part of Lady Bracknell. I concede. 'OK,' I say. 'Love's an illusion.' I've heard that somewhere. To agree with Mel is the best way to call her bluff, sometimes. She looks at me. It's her other look, the opposite of her far-away one. She has unusual eyes – flecked, the iris blue and green and grey and gold and each colour distinct; the white part is very white. Mel's eyes are her best feature. But when she looks at you this way you stop noticing her eyes, as though you can see past them to a small secret place where the real Mel lives. She doesn't let you in very often, which is only natural.

'Gabriel? You don't really think that's true, do you?'

'I hope it isn't true,' I tell her honestly.

'I hope it isn't too,' she says. The game is over. We're in agreement, which we usually are though we like to pretend. We go down to the pool for a swim.

The pool is new. For two years we've had raffles and class fund-raising contests and limp fudge cake from the school tuck-shop, sixpence the piece. And now we have a swimming pool.

Mel and I stand beside the steps that lead down to the water, eau-de-Nil water that reminds me of polar seas, lapping on smooth tiles white as ice floes. My bathing-suit is regulation black and my skin is very pale.

I tried to tan last year when Mel and I went camping with her cousins. The tan stayed for two days and peeled away, like dirt. All that stayed in my skin was the smell of sunshine when I breathed on my arm. We kept to ourselves in our ten-by-ten canvas world and waited for sunburnt boys to pay court. We wore eyeshadow, and four changes of beachwear every day. The boys went by our tent and we noticed that the girls beside them looked like Ann, who never wore eyeshadow, and said 'some-think'. We were not grateful to Ann for taking us camping, in the same way that we were not grateful to our parents for conceiving us in their middle age. We did not think about it. Mel and I did not talk about the boys. We bought chocolate-dipped ice-creams, and walked along the beach with our heads close together to hear over the wind and surf.

The light went quickly one evening when we were still on the beach. The two boys came silently out of the sandhills so that at first we were startled. We walked, the four of us, towards the rocks at the end of the beach, together at first, later in pairs, Mel and her boy ahead. His walk was almost a shamble; his arms, before he put one round her shoulders, swung loosely. Smugly, I felt sorry for Mel. The boy beside me was tall and his hand felt firm and warm. It grew dark, and I could have walked on to the rocks for ever.

Mel and her boy drew further ahead as we turned back and went towards the dunes. I wished that Mel was following to notice that my boy didn't shamble and was tall. The juice of the succulent plants, closed now against night, ran out between my toes as he turned me to him and kissed me. His lips, like his palms, were dry and warm. But then his tongue was terrible, slithering wet, strong, a dark eel belonging under stones in the river. He held me tightly but I pulled away and ran back, on and on, to the camp, to the tent. My chest hurt with fright and

running. I waited for Mel and was angry because she hadn't
stayed with me.

She came back soon. I was curious to know if she had been
kissed by her boy but she didn't say and I didn't like to ask. Nor
did I tell her about the kiss that had made me afraid. I knew I had
not behaved with sophistication, although my eyeshadow was
silver and glistened under light. We went to bed soon, on the
double mattress that Ann had brought on the trailer for us.
Mel's warmth, her solidity, the faint spicy smell of her hair near
my face comforted me and I feel asleep against her.

Holidays end; school brings back the pleasures of challenge,
approval, Mel's company. We vie in class. While other girls form
friendly circles at lunchtime, Mel and I sit apart. In wet weather
the shelter sheds smell of sour milk and sandshoes, and wasps
hang around the overflowing rubbish tins. When it's fine we sit
under the gum trees, and sometimes after lunch we go for a
swim.

I look at the pale water, and think that I'm not a good swimmer,
that I don't like cold water, that I don't want to go in. Mel, beside
me, reaches out and touches a finger behind my shoulders. 'You
have such a smooth back,' she says, sounding surprised as
though she's just noticed something. Compliments are unusual:
from adults who are watchful of praise, from Mel, who tries as I
do to be adult. Her words sink like smooth pebbles to the bottom
of my thoughts; later I will take them out, turn them over, fondle
them. I am flattered. I am happy. I leap suddenly into the water
and without a single rest I swim a full width of the pool.

After school we catch the bus to town. It is Friday afternoon,
the first Friday of the month. Mel and I are making the Nine
First Fridays, in honour of the Sacred Heart. When we have
finished we shall be certain of going to heaven; as promised to St
Margaret-Mary by the Lord Himself we shall be allowed the
grace of final repentance on our deathbeds. Death seems
beyond us, as impossible as the committing of horrible, mortal
sin, but then one never knows. The Nine Fridays may save us in

the final count. Mass and Communion for nine consecutive
First Fridays of the month is a little price to pay for heaven.
Besides, before Mass at seven o'clock, there's afternoon tea and
a five o'clock session of the pictures. We never see the end of the
film because we can't be late for Mass. It doesn't matter a lot.
We make up our own endings.

Mel's watch is fast. We are early for Mass. Men and women
tread quietly past the confessional boxes into the great cave of
the church. Confessional doors open and close; voices too
muted to understand exchange private words as Mel and I,
kneeling together, examine our consciences. HailHolyQueen.
HailOurLifeOurSweetnessAndHope. ToTheeDoWeCome.
BeforeTheeWeStand. SinfulAndSorrowful. Sinful. Even the
just man falls seven times daily. Why so hard to put together a
respectable list for Father who waits gravely in there, in the
small cave smelling so strongly of old planed wood? His profile
beneath the dim bulb appears as the window slides back. Latin
phrases of absolution switch suddenly, like light, to the patient,
'Yes, my child?' My child? Can he see me? How does he know
this is not an old woman, a murderer, a sinner come to
repentance after thirty years? Oh, to have the choice of thirty
years' wickedness from which to pick sins like cans from a
supermarket shelf; oh, how disappointing a display of sin.
Disobeyed Mother. Several times. Told lies twice. No. Not
harmful to anyone. Not calumny. One about the music practice.
One about the chocolates. Mother knew anyway. 'And anything
else?' Anything else, anything else . . . Surely, surely, *something*?
Answered back, but she deserved that. I answered back, Father.
Impure thoughts? Had an impure thought. 'Yes, my child. I see.
And anything else now?' Anything else anything else Father I'm
almost wetting my pants because it's so dark and there's nothing
else so please give me my penance – a thought only, unspoken.
Would that be a sin, to do that in Confession? Surely not, not
even there. Has anyone ever? . . . dear child, pray for help, Our
Blessed Mother, temptation is no sin, remember that the Devil

tempted Christ Himself in the desert . . . Yes Father. Pray my child. Yes Father. You do remember your prayers always? Mostly Father. 'I see, my child. And nothing else?'

When I was small I used to clutch when I felt I couldn't wait and Mother would say don't, Gabriel, don't do that. Nice little girls don't do that. I do it now, praying that Father can't see, praying there won't be a little trail of wetness left behind on the brown linoleum when I emerge, absolved, into the light.

For your penance three Hail Marys, and now a good Act of Contrition. OhMyGodIAmVerySorryThatIHaveSinned Against Thee. BecauseThouArtSoGood. AndIWillNotSin-Again. Amen. *Te absolvo*. Thank you, Father. The window closes.

I open the door, go back to the church and the faces looking up from their conscience-stricken hunting. Have I been a long time? Too long? Fall gratefully, blushing, into any pew. Disappear. A light-headed feeling of freedom like the last day of term. Sin all gone. Sorrowful? Happy. Bury eyes down on to clasped hands. Three Hail Marys, one, two, three. A soul now, round and white as a peppermint, the smuts of sin rubbed out. Gabriel shriven.

Most people leave as soon as Mass is over. Mel and I stay behind, kneeling side by side. The church is a great high cave where we are together, lost, alone. The candles sparkling on the side altar remind me of glow-worms high up on the caves at Waitomo, cold caves, dark, with lapping black water sensed more than seen. 'My, now *this* is *something*!' the American woman says, impressed again. I think of black sky, no moon, the death of a star, and I am glad to climb the rickety wooden steps up to the light again. Caves are sinister places, running back to no-exits of darkness and dripping water. Mel isn't afraid of caves. She is practical. She will be saying the fourth decade of the rosary and planning her weekend essay. Her beads move, tapping lightly the polished pew cut with the initials J.B., rayed round with lines like a child's sun.

The church smells warmly of flowers and incense. I ease my

weight to one knee, to the other, and rest my face against my bent arms. It's no good. I give in and sit down, tracing through the lisle stockings the deep indentations that mark each knee. Mel's back rises straight and rigid as the brown-robed St Joseph who gazes past us from his niche. His head does not wear a beret, but clustered curls and a plaster beard, set stiffly on his chin like old spaghetti. Looking at Mel I am ashamed. I kneel down again, notice the blunt renewed ache in my knees and the warmth of Mel beside me. Her blazer filters a musky smell like faded incense. Hail Holy Queen Mother Of Mercy. Hail Our Life Our Sweetness And Our Hope. To Thee Do We Come. Before Thee We Stand. Sinful And Sorrowful.

Grateful when Mel's nudge comes, I stand up stiffly, like the old women who wear headscarves and chew on their prayers without caring who listens in to their conversations with the Lord. How sad, I think, how impossible to ever be old like that. I follow Mel down the side aisle, my legs forgetting their stiffness, my callous soul ignoring the sad dimmed oil paintings of the Way of the Cross. Dip, splash, the holy water font an ivory shell. Catholic Truth Society pamphlets, red, blue, purple, on the rack in the church porch. *Have you a vocation? Sacramental Grace. Youth and Problems of Purity.* I cannot go and take that title out of the rack, not with Mel or somebody to see me and wonder why I'm buying that one; but it sounds more interesting than *Fallacies of Jansenism.* We pass the pamphlets and go outside. It is March and by eight o'clock night has settled down cosily. I was sleepy in the warm church. Now, feeling the thin cold air trickle through my nose, I am suddenly wide awake, and pleased with myself.

'Well, that's eight,' I say.

'Eight what? Oh, you mean Fridays.'

'Only one to go. Did you think we'd really do it, Mel?'

'We haven't yet. There's one more, remember.'

Sometimes I find Mel's precision annoying, but I don't mind tonight. What does it matter? Mel is coming to stay the night and I am happy.

We have never been less tired than we are now, at bedtime.

'Straight off to sleep now,' Mother says firmly, hopefully. In the darkness I sense Mel in the other bed. We talk in whispers, muffling giggles in our pillows.

'Mel? You know when we were up at the beach last summer, and you went down to the rocks with that boy?'

'The one with the acne? The friendly monster from outer space?'

'He wasn't *that* bad.'

'He was. You were jolly pleased the other one picked you.'

'I was not.'

'Yes, you were. He was a crumb.'

'Yes, but did he . . . did you . . .?'

'What?'

'Oh *you* know.'

'For heaven's sake!'

'Did you, well, kiss him?'

'*He* did. I didn't.'

'Didn't you like it?'

'No. I don't think so. It was wet.'

'Was it? So was mine. All sloppy. He just about stuck his tongue down my throat.'

'Mine didn't do that. He kind of chewed, like those old men who don't wear their teeth.'

'Ugh.'

'Yuck.'

Exquisitely funny. We scream silently into our pillows.

'Licking ice-cream.'

'Slurping soup.'

'Gob-stoppers in your mouth. *Two*.'

Excruciating. We roll on our stomachs, hysterical. We have forgotten that Mother, in the next room, is tired and is trying to have an early night. Bang of the wall. Bangbang. Stop that noise, girls. Off to sleep. At once.

Silence.

'Gabriel?'

'Ssshh! She'll hear. Come over here.'

Mel in blue pyjamas brings her incense smell into my bed. We arrange ourselves together, bump to hollow, hollow to bump. 'Gabriel? What do you think about it? You know what I mean. Did your mother tell you or what?'

'She told me. Did your mother?'

'She gave me a book. Last year.'

A whole book! My information had been received in the five minutes between rosary and night prayers.

'What was it like?'

'Awful drawings.'

'Like biology class?'

'Worse. There wasn't much about it. The actual part. It had a lot about getting pregnant and how not to and diseases and that.'

Disappointing. I thought there might be something Mother had forgotten about. What she had told me had seemed really rather pointless.

'Mel? Didn't you think it sounded silly? I mean, don't you wonder why people *do* it?'

'It sounds mad, I think. Don't ask me. You'd think they'd have a better system, wouldn't you? An incubator plant or something.'

'Yes. I think it sounds awful.'

'Well I'm not going to do it anyway. Ever.'

'Neither am I.'

Is it incense, powder, faint sun-on-skin perspiration, this special warm smell that is Mel? The winceyette cloth of her pyjama coat has rubbed into tiny balls under my fingers. I am alive. I quicken with awareness like the vibration of a single hair when we sit, heads not quite touching, in the pictures. I will change my mind and be embarrassed, so I say it quickly before I have time to think. 'Mel,' I say, 'I do like you.'

She turns her head back as though she hasn't heard me. The toothpaste on her breath reminds me of the pink smokers we buy in cellophane packets as she answers.

'Well I like you,' she says. I am happy. I find her lowest rib and tickle. We have forgotten again. Bang. Bangbangbang.

'Get to SLEEP!'

Silence.

'Mel?'

'What?'

'I thought you were asleep.'

'No.'

'Oh.'

At the back of her neck, in the hollow, the hair is fine, like a baby's. I feel it for an instant, lighter than a touch on my lips, and wonder if I imagine its softness.

'G'night, Mel.'

'Mmhmm. G'night.'

Then it is morning and Mother is standing by the bed, wearing her least-pleased expression. We stumble up from sleep and go in dressing-gowns to the kitchen for breakfast. The air is thick with Mother's bad mood and fumes from the kerosene heater. Our plates are whisked away, dealt ferociously into the sink. The silence trembles with crashes. I ask with guilt if I can dry.

'Don't bother yourself,' Mother says, passing the tea-towel to me. 'You go and enjoy yourself with your friend. Don't think of your mother.'

'Didn't you have a good night?' I ask foolishly. Mother snatches her trump.

'Good night? Good *night*? The pair of you talking and giggling half the night . . . My word, wait till you're my age. Young people are selfish today. Very selfish.' I dry in silence.

'Is it all right if Mel and I do some homework now?'

'Do as you like. Don't bother to ask me what you can do or can't do. You'll do what you please. You're just like your father.'

I go back to the bedroom. Mel is dressed. 'What's the matter with your mother. Isn't she feeling well?'

'Oh,' I say vaguely, 'she gets like that. She didn't have a very

good night or something.' It does not seem reasonable that
Mother's sleep is dependent on my own. A heavy burden.

Homework is done. Mother is ironing.

'Mel wants me to go over to her place. Can I?' I ask.

'You and that girl are always in each other's pocket,' Mother
says with resentment. 'If it's not her coming to our place it's you
wanting to go there. I don't know what her mother thinks, I'm
sure.' It hasn't occurred to me that Mel's mother thinks at all.
She is a doing person, never still, always washing, ironing, busy
in the kitchen. She uses the weekends to catch up on the week
when she's away at work.

'We have to finish this project on pollution by Monday, and
Mel's got a book about it.' (BlessMeFather, I told one lie.)

'Go if you must,' says Mother, branding Father's shirt with a
vicious stab. 'Please yourself. If her mother can put up with your
nonsense and carrying on, go. It makes no difference to me.
What I'd like to know is, where are all those nice little friends
you used to have to your birthdays, that nice little what's-her-
name, Rosemary, Mary Rose, what's happened to her?'

I am patient. 'Mother, that was years ago. Absolute ages.
She's gone all stupid now. All she talks about is boys.'

'There's worse than boys,' says my mother, thumping the iron
fast. 'A lot worse. You want to think about that, my girl.'

'What d'you mean?' I ask. The damping-bottle flies, sprink-
ling me with drops, like holy water from the Benediction
procession.

'I'll tell you what I'm talking about; you see far too much of
that girl, that's what I'm talking about. In case you don't know it
there are some funny people about, very funny men, and funny
women too, and no girl of mine is growing up into one of them.
That's what I'm talking about.'

'I don't know what you mean,' I say. 'I don't understand you.'

'I hope you don't,' she says, and says no more, for she has
looked at me and seen my face and I think she is sorry that she let
her tiredness and her oldness make her say that, that way. But I

think also that she is glad it has been said. At least that is what I decide, later on. As I turn and run away out of the kitchen, into the bathroom, lock the door, sit on the edge of the bath, let the hot hot tears run down, I understand nothing, and everything, and I feel sick to my heart. A grey web of guilt is spinning itself about me. For the first time in my life I learn what it is to be quite alone.

Mel and I go to town. We have afternoon tea. We go to the pictures. We go to church, and kneel side by side. The doors of the confessionals open, close; inaudible words murmur a thread of melody. Mel leaves me and closes the door behind her.

Bless me, Father, for I have sinned. Anything else, my child? Anything else? Sin unspoken makes a worse sin, the sin of deceit, for the priest is the ear of God. Have I sinned? I remember the softness of old winceyette, the fineness of young hair at the back of the neck, in the hollow.

Mel comes out, composed as always. 'I'm not going,' I say. And I turn my back on her surprised face and walk up the church away from the confessionals.

The Ninth Friday. Nine consecutive First Fridays and nine communions and heaven is a promise. This is My Body. And This is My Blood. Mel goes up to receive communion. I do not go. I stay in my seat, kneeling very straight, and I try to concentrate on the pain in my knees and not think of the other pain. I have not made the Nine Fridays and I am trying not to cry.

. . . *But Not By Dirt* . . .

LEONORA BRITO

June. Our front garden is filled with potato plants. Spriggly and deep dark green. I feel misery inside me when I think of those potato plants out there in our front like that. My father went and planted them there, after Mr Blueser had dug up the ground first. Mr Blueser is a skinny man, the colour of a used coin. He has wild staring eyes and can't speak properly. He tried to say 'thank you' when I brought him a glass of water, but the jugular veins moved up and down in his neck like pulleys, mangling the sounds that came out.

My father paid him ten shillings for the job and fed him beans and rice. He ate quickly, bulging his cheeks like Popeye and staring straight ahead of him. Still you could see Mr Blueser's rib-cage, like the inside of an upturned rowing-boat pressed against the soft grey of his vest. Poor Blueser, he's going home soon, the government said they'd help him with his passage and send his old-age pension out to him every three months. He dug up the garden good though, and when he'd finished raking it over, I went and stood near the edge of the concrete path and looked. The red brown of the earth had crumbled into absolute evenness; you could fill your eyes with it. And no matter how many times I looked, there was nothing in that small square of earth that was out of place.

How long ago was that? I hate the deadness of Sunday evenings like this. The main road is quiet; the two bus-stops are empty. Every now and again, posses of stray dogs trot along the pavement, heading up, moving out. I'm fed up with this place. Everything is effing gladioli, tulips and hedges. Apart from next-door's lavatory bowl still outside their front, waiting for the council to come and collect it; and that mass of vegetation growing in ours. I don't know! And how come it's poor Blueser who's going somewhere? And why is my father planting potatoes? I ask myself as I turn from the window.

I lie down on the bed and take one gold stud from my ear-lobe. I bring my face up close to the ball-bearing end. From far and away, my face blazes into a kind of brightness, jonquil yellow, hedged by a couple of wintry-looking bushes, artificially shaped. I, Marcia Angela Tobin, am fourteen years of age. What does that mean? Anything? Yet I've noticed myself becoming more and more detective lately. I watch everyone closely. I play tape-recordings in my head all the time. And I realize things.

Take my father for instance. Lionel. At this very moment he is sat downstairs in the front room waiting for half past seven, because he's on nights this week, and nights begin on Sundays. He'll be sitting up straight, though the settee is low and soft-cushioned. His working face is iron dark and unfathomable. Search me, I say to myself, using two or three different voices, search me.

He shouts my name from the foot of the stairs, just before he is ready to go. I yell back 'What!' but my feet move quickly towards the banister to deaden the force of what I say. He issues instructions while counting over his bus fare. My father is a man who counts and counts. I know what he will say before he has said it. That the back-door is locked eh, and make sure you bolt this one after me, you hear? and to remember, anyone knock, you doan answer. He raises his head from his counting, 'You hear me?' I have seen the patina of his face on old coins. 'Eh?'

When the door slams shut, I wait for the clang of the gate, but his voice blasts through the letter-box to make me jump. 'Bolt this door now, while I'm here.' Me fadder never treat me like a chile, to him always I am big ana stupid. But sometimes I know it is to do with him being a man and having to bring up a girl child on his own. Is it the man's fault I have fourteen year an too big already for me age? And too, his own self gradually shrinkin . . .

I wander over to the sideboard, picking things up and putting them back down again. My hands close around two glass paper weights, very smooth and cold. I shake them up and down like a pair of maracas. Kicking up a snow storm inside the dark blue light. Lionel brought them back from sea, Genoa. I watch the snowflakes settle at the bottom of each glass, the skies are a clear romantic blue over beaches made of desiccated coconut. Nat King Cole comes into my head, he wears my father's pink calypso shirt and he sings a slow song. His pronunciation is *demnably* correct. I sing the same and shake the maracas over and over. 'They just lie there, *end*. They die there . . . do you smile –' Christ I'm a kid. I am not a kid. Put them down. Get on with your work. Righto. Look, whose voice dis is? Look, the blue of the glass has tinged the brownness of my one hand green . . .

They stare at me from their wedding photo on the mantelpiece, their doubled eyes, uncomprehending. I pick up the photograph and tilt it towards the light. A snowy morning in April, hand tinted. Lionel is hued in dark browns with slashes here and there of bronze. The snowflakes are like thick wisps of cotton wool, all falling at a slant, the colouring on my mother's lips is the only spot of vividness about her. I tilt the picture more sharply, sometimes I fancy the images are fading, though I keep them in my head, two figures in black and white.

This morning first thing, I looked out through the window. I note the greenery creeping up and up. We'll be knee-deep soon. As if I cared . . . Last night I listened to the radiogram and this morning I have two new songs to take to school. Once I'm in school I put on a hard face. I hate the teachers, in particular Stanley (who we call the ring-master) and Mary (the elephant). Break-time, I move from group to group, selling my father's duty-free cigarettes, brought by a friend, a compadre, from sea. I'm making money, it's so easy it fascinates me. I'm saving up. I catch bits of conversation:

'He didn't want Butler, he wanted top.'

'She gave him top, she gave him top.'

'And bottom.'

'No, no she never, only top.'

There's a silence before everyone laughs. It surprises me. To see how hard they are, and Butler supposed to be their friend. I keep the surprise out of my face, I'm a black marketeer. They cluster round my twenty cigarettes, I allow them to finger the gold writing on the outside of the carton. Someone asks me where I got them from. 'Stole'm,' I say quickly and they laugh.

Afterwards I give Jane and Andrea a cigarette each. Andrea tells me about Melvin as she smokes it. It's always me she tells, ever since she started going out with him four weeks ago. It's made her more friends with me, somehow. After bursting into the classroom one day, one of the first summery kind of days, they were all smiles, the two of them and whispering across the desks:

'Do you . . . know a boy called Melvin?'

I had shaken my head.

'You must do, he's a culluboy . . . he's not your cousin or something?'

'Dopes!'

But the two of them were smiling so childish, like if something wonderful and exciting was happening; and it was one of the first summery kind of days, so that I had to laugh too.

Now I listen to Andrea while I stack my money away in little piles. They want four kids, two boys and two girls. The little girls will be called Jade and Amber. Jane pulls a face and so do I, trying to picture Jade and Amber. Then Andrea pulls a face when she sees us starting to laugh. 'Orr! doan you like those names, doan you? I think they're gorgeous, for little girls I do . . .' She shoves at my shoulder as we move towards the lines, I forget to ask about the boys' names.

July. I've been mitching off from school. I can't stand it there. The others moan, but they don't hate. I'm on my own. Mary the elephant tried to find out what was wrong. She calls me Carmel. 'Now just what *is* the matter with you Carmel, hm? You seem to have developed a real chip on your shoulder, would you like to tell me about it, dear?' I just stared at her until she got nasty and sent me away. Course I'd known all along she was putting it on.

If it's a nice day I sit in the park, enjoying the sunshine on my arms and legs. Old posh people sit on benches and contemplate the flowers lined up, row after row in front of them. These benches are hard. Mothers allow their pestering kids to climb up on the wooden slats, then shake them when they fall and start to cry. I watch them wheel the crying kids away, speeding along, then slowing down, speeding along, slowing down, until the kids forget and start to laugh.

Click. Her face never comes into focus properly. It's like cold water blurring up in your eye. Enormous. You blink and it's gone. Except that I can remember the feel of her fingers moving in my hair, combing and parting her way through as if it were an undergrowth. 'Let me see you with this piece in the front,' she said. When I turned to face her, she shook her head. 'Turn back round, let's try it like this.' 'And keep still!' she always said. 'Keep still or I'll leave it like it is.'

The butcher's shop had a red and white coldness about it with flashes of silver and bright green parsley. The butcher's wife wraps up the meat in a triangle of kitchen paper, quickly before the blood seeps through. Then she reaches over the counter to touch my hair with her cold reddened fingers, 'Look Bill,' she says, 'lambs tails.'

Sunlight presses on my eyelids like a band, when I open them I have to blink hard before I can see. I make my way out of the park at four o'clock, and walk towards the ornamental gates. When I was eight, I used to tell her everything, stand by the bed and tell her, 'Mama these two boys said they'd beat me up, Ma, kids are callin me blackie alla time, nigger, wog, Ma?'

And what did she use to say? Plenty, and call me daft for being soft and I used to feel better and ready for the next time, though I noticed, when she stood and walked slowly towards the stairs, that the calves of her legs were white, as white as the packs of lard in the butcher's shop.

I trail my finger along the iron railings, grass and flowers in vertical strips, that's all I can see as I go along, nature, clipped and dull. Then I think of my nature, *my own nature* and that fills up my head like a garden of flourishing chlorophyll green. Outside the park gates there are men waiting in cars. I remember the first time one of them leaned across the steering wheel and told me to get in. All I did was stare at him and he stared back like if it was nothing, like opening the door to the rent man or the insurance man. Now if one of them said anything, I'd just tell him to eff off. I'd say, 'Eff off you shrimp-arsed git,' and I'd say it over my shoulder as I crossed the road. But I always wonder, why do they think I'd get in the car with them? Do I look as if I'd jump into a car? With them? I would never tell him at home, he'd make too much fuss.

Walking up the garden path I notice that some of the potato plants have flowered, tiny pale yellow flowers, I kick at the heads as I go past.

My father is talking about me to Mr Talbot in the front room. I hold the tin-opener in my hand and listen. I can't really catch what he says, but it's something about me singing. It's true I've taken to singing, but I don't want Mr Talbot and all of them to know that. Mr Talbot is big and fat, I twist the metal butterfly on the side of the tin-opener. I think of Mr Talbot as a twister twisting things, twisting out of things. He makes it his business to stand on the front porch and inspect the potato patch at the end of every visit, all the while nodding and smiling in admiration. Mr Talbot's own front garden has a lawn and a small rockery with a statue of Our Lady Star of the Sea in the middle of it.

'Kids!' I hear him say, and he gives a small laugh. I can imagine him mopping his head with a large white handkerchief. 'Always this pop, pop, pop, my Johnny the same but you know, teacher to tell me that boy could a go to university, that is to say Ox-ford, Cam-bridge . . .' There is a small silence, then my father mentions the horses, 'You have any luck? Me neither, notta shit . . .'

I remember back to when him and Mr Talbot were big men, home from sea. My father would pour out small tots of rum and the two of them would sit and talk seriously. They would always ignore the plates of cake and biscuits at their side. Men don't eat sweet things when they're with other men, I think to myself and marvel as I scoop the tuna fish on to a plate.

When I take the tray into the room, Mr Talbot breaks off in the middle of what he's saying. He smiles broadly as he takes his cup, 'When you ready to give us a song then, eh?' His smile takes in my father on the other side of the room. I notice Mr Talbot's gold side teeth, they seem to have a dull, tin soft gleam about them. My face is empty. 'Shy!' says Mr Talbot, he throws back his head and laughs. I glimpse the roof of his mouth indented all the way down like a polished mackerel bone.

August. The front garden is empty. All the green stalks have been cleared away, burnt in a heap; the thick-skinned potatoes have been piled up and stored in a sack under the staircase. We worked as a team and at the end of the day, my father began to talk about next year. 'Next year,' he said, 'if god spare you . . .' As soon as he said that I stopped listening and concentrated on cleaning the dirt from my fingernails.

My arms have been blackened by the sun, but only up to the elbows, like evening gloves. In idle moments like these, I picture myself gliding across a stage grandly, my hair palmed down by coconut oil . . . But how you supposed to look? I spent the cigarette money on make-up and a ruched top which had hundreds of gold threads running through it. Andrea went with me to the shops. When she saw my face with the make-up on she drew back and said, 'My god Marcia! You looks white with the make-up you do!'

'Oh piss off,' I'd said laughing and scrubbing at my face with a tissue. 'I doan wanna look like none of you lot.' But Andrea shushed me as if I were a small child. 'Now doan be silly of course you do, course you do Marcie . . .'

When I tried the top on properly at home, I didn't like the feel of it, dry and scaled like snakeskin, that's me out as a singer in those long tight glittery evening gowns. Then I picked at the gold threads, unravelling them one by one. Rice threads are cheap, some of the gold came off in my hands, and I kept glancing down at them because I fancied they showed a green tinge. Like when you're a kid and you keep money in your hands too long it smudges them green and it's hard to get off.

After the garden was cleared, I tried raking it over, but it didn't look the same as when Mr Blueser did it. The soil is too dry now, and pebbly looking. When I think of Mr Blueser, I always think of the country blues; and I imagine Mr Blueser as an itinerant, country blues man. And that is really daft because I know now that 'Blueser' is really spelt 'Blusa'. That's what he bought one trip to South America, a woman's blouse. Mr Talbot and my father have talked about how he used to wear it all the time until they forced him to see what it was. 'Chow man for shame! get rid on dem bloody girl ting.' Mr Talbot says the government will never increase poor Blueser's pension, doan matter how much contribution he paid in over the years. 'Tacoma Star torpedo off in the war an alla that, no dem use . . .'

This summer, my body looks as if it's been mapped out in different colours, a black, a gold and a brown. And my hair, after it's been washed, springs up from my head like a rain-forest, the whirr of an insect makes me think of a helicopter surveying the Amazon forests below it. It seems funny to be thinking of a continent, when you've always been brought up on an island . . .

Beg, Sl Tog, Inc, Cont, Rep

AMY HEMPEL

The mohair was scratchy, the stria too bulky, but the homespun tweed was right for a small frame. I bought slate-blue skeins softened with flecks of pink, and size 10 needles for a sweater that was warm but light. The pattern I chose was a two-tone V-neck with an optional six-stitch cable up the front. Pullovers mess the hair, but I did not want to buttonhole the first time out.

From a needlework book, I learned to cast on. In the test piece, I got the gauge and correct tension. Knit and purl came naturally, as though my fingers had been rubbed in spiderwebs at birth. The sliding of the needles was as rhythmic as water.

Learning to knit was the obvious thing. The separation of tangled threads, the working together of ravelled ends into something tangible and whole – this *mending* was as confounding as the groom who drives into a stop sign on the way to his wedding. Because symptoms mean just what they are. What about the woman whose empty hand won't close because she cannot grasp that her child is gone?

'Would you get me a Dr Pep, gal, and would you turn up the a-c?'

I put down my knitting. In the kitchen I found some sugar-free, and took it, with ice, to Dale Anne. It was August. Air-conditioning lifted her hair as she pressed the button on the Niagara bed. Dr Diamond insisted she have it the last month. She was also renting a swivel TV table and a vibrating chaise – the Niagara adjustable home.

When the angle was right, she popped a Vitamin E and rubbed the oil where the stretch marks would be.

I could be doing this, too. But I had had the procedure instead. That was after the father had asked me, Was I sure? To his credit, he meant – sure that I *was*, not sure was it he. He said he had never made a girl pregnant before. He said that he had never even made a girl late.

I moved in with Dale Anne to help her near the end. Her husband is often away – in a clinic or in a lab. He studies the mind. He is not a doctor yet, but we call him one by way of encouragement.

I had picked up a hank of yarn and was winding it into a ball when the air-conditioner choked to a stop.

Dale Anne sighed. 'I will *cook* in this robe. Would you get me that flowered top in the second drawer?'

While I looked for the top, Dale Anne twisted her hair and held it tight against her head. She took one of my double-pointed six-inch needles and wove it in and out of her hair, securing the twist against her scalp. With the hair off her face, she looked wholesome and very young – 'the person you would most like to go camping with if you couldn't have sex', is how she put it.

I turned my back while Dale Anne changed. She was as modest as I was. If the house caught fire one night, we would both die struggling to hook brassières beneath our gowns.

I went back to my chair, and as I did, a sensational cramp snapped me over until I was nearly on the floor.

'Easy, gal – what's the trouble?' Dale Anne started out of bed to come see.

I said it sometimes happens since the procedure, and Dale Anne said, 'Let's not talk about that for at *least* ten years.'

I could not think of what to say to that. But I didn't have to. The front door opened, earlier than it usually did. It was Dr Diamond, home from the world of spooks and ghosts and loony bins and Ouija boards. I knew that a lack of concern for others was a hallmark of mental illness, so I straightened up and said, after he'd kissed his pregnant wife, 'You look hot, Dr Diamond. Can I get you a drink?'

I buy my materials at a place in the residential section. The owner's name is Ingrid. She is a large Norwegian woman who spells needles 'kneedles'. She wears sample knits she makes up for the class demonstrations. The vest she wore the day before will be hanging in the window.

There are always four or five women at Ingrid's round oak table, knitting through a stretch they would not risk alone.

Often I go there when I don't need a thing. In the small back room that is stacked high with pattern books, I can sift for hours. I scan the instructions abbreviated like musical notation: *K10, sl I, K2 tog, psso, sl I, K10 to end.* I feel I could *sing* these instructions. It is compression of language into code; your ability to decipher it makes you privy to the secrets shared by Ingrid and the women at the round oak table.

In the other room, Ingrid tells a customer she used to knit two hundred stitches a minute.

I scan the French and English catalogues, noting the longer length of coat. There is so much to absorb on each visit.

Mary had a little lamb, I am humming when I leave the shop. *Its feet were – its fleece was white as wool.*

Dale Anne wanted a nap, so Dr Diamond and I went out for margaritas. At La Rondalla, the coloured lights on the Virgin tell you every day is Christmas. The food arrives on manhole covers and mariachis fill the bar. Dr Diamond said that in Guadalajara there is a mariachi college that turns out mariachis by the classful. But I could tell that these were not graduates of even mariachi high school.

I shooed the serenaders away, but Dr Diamond said they meant well.

Dr Diamond likes for people to mean well. He could be president of the Well-Meaning Club. He has had a buoyant feeling of fate since he learned Freud died the day he was born.

He was the person to talk to, all right, so I brought up the stomach pains I was having for no bodily reason that I could think of.

'You know how I think,' he said. 'What is it you can't stomach?'

I knew what he was asking.

'Have you thought about how you will feel when Dale Anne has the baby?' he asked.

With my eyes, I wove strands of tinsel over the Blessed Virgin. That was the great thing about knitting, I thought – everything was fibre, the world a world of natural resource.

'I thought I would burn that bridge when I come to it,' I said, and when he didn't say anything to that, I said, 'I guess I will think that there is a mother who *kept* hers.'

'*One* of hers might be more accurate,' Dr Diamond said.

I arrived at the yarn shop as Ingrid turned over the *Closed* sign to *Open*. I had come to buy Shetland wool for a Fair Isle sweater. I felt nothing would engage my full attention more than a pattern of ancient Scottish symbols and alternate bands of delicate design. Every stitch in every colour is related to the one above, below, and to either side.

I chose the natural colours of Shetland sheep – the chalky brown of the Moorit, the blackish brown of the black sheep, fawn, grey, and pinky beige from a mixture of Moorit and white. I held the wool to my nose, but Ingrid said it was fifty years since the women of Fair Isle dressed the yarn with fish oil.

She said the yarn came from Sheep Rock, the best pasture on Fair Isle. It is a ten-acre plot that is four hundred feet up a cliff, Ingrid said. 'Think what a man has to go through to harvest the wool.'

I was willing to feel an obligation to the yarn, and to the hardy Scots who supplied it. There was heritage there, and I could keep it alive with my hands.

Dale Anne patted capers into a mound of raw beef, and spread some on to toast. It was not a pretty sight. She offered some to me, and I said not a chance. I told her Johnny Carson is someone else who won't go near that. I said, 'Johnny says he won't eat steak tartare because he has seen things hurt worse than that get better.'

'Johnny was never pregnant,' Dale Anne said.

When the contractions began, I left a message with the hospital and with Dr Diamond's lab. I turned off the air-conditioner and called for a cab.

'Look at you,' Dale Anne said.

I told her I couldn't help it. I get rational when I panic.

The taxi came in minutes.

'Hold on,' the driver said. 'I know every bump in these roads, and I've never been able to miss one of them.'

Dale Anne tried to squeeze my wrist, but her touch was weightless, as porous as wet silk.

'When this is over . . .' Dale Anne said.

When the baby was born, I did not go far. I sublet a place on the other side of town. I filled it with patterns and needles and yarn. It was what I did in the day. On a good day, I made a front and two sleeves. On a bad day, I ripped out stitches from neck to hem. For variety, I made socks. The best ones I made had beer steins on the sides, and the tops spilled over with white angora foam.

I did not like to work with sound in the room, not even the sound of a fan. Music slowed me down, and there was a great deal to do. I planned to knit myself a mailbox and a car, perhaps even a dog and a lead to walk him.

I blocked the finished pieces and folded them in drawers.

Dr Diamond urged me to exercise. He called from time to time, looking in. He said exercise would set me straight, and why not have some fun with it? Why not, for example, tap-dancing lessons?

I told him it would be embarrassing because the rest of the

class would be doing it right. And with all the knitting, there wasn't time to dance.

Dale Anne did not look in. She had a pretty good reason not to.

The day I went to see her in the hospital, I stopped at the nursery first. I saw the baby lying face down. He wore yellow duck-print flannels. I saw that he was there – and then I went straight home.

That night the dreams began. A giant lizard ate people from the feet upwards, swallowing the argyles on the first bite, then drifting into obscurity like a ranger of forgotten death. I woke up remembering and, like a chameleon, assumed every shade of blame.

Asleep at night, I went to an elegant ball. In the centre of the dance floor was a giant aquarium. Hundreds of goldfish swam inside. At a sign from the bandleader, the tank was overturned. Until someone tried to dance on the fish, the floor was aswirl with gold glory.

Dr Diamond told a story about the young daughter of a friend. The little girl had found a frog in the yard. The frog appeared to be dead, so her parents let her prepare a burial site – a little hole surrounded by pebbles. But at the moment of the lowering, the frog, which had only been stunned, kicked its legs and came to.

'Kill him!' the girl had shrieked.

I began to take walks in the park. In the park, I saw a dog try to eat his own shadow, and another dog – I am sure of it – was herding a stand of elms. I stopped telling people how handsome their dogs were; too many times what they said was, 'You want him?'

When the weather got nicer, I stayed home to sit for hours. I had accidents. Then I had bigger ones. But the part that hurt was never the part that got hurt.

The dreams came back and back until they were just – again. I wished that things would stay out of sight the way they did in mountain lakes. In one that I know, the water is so cold, gas can't form to bring a corpse to the surface. Although you would not want to think about the bottom of the lake, what you can say about it is – the dead stay down.

Around that time I talked to Dr Diamond.

The point that he wanted to make was this: that conception was not like walking in front of traffic. No matter how badly timed, it was, he said, an affirmation of life.

'You have to believe me here,' he said. 'Do you see that this is true? Do you know this about yourself?'

'I do and I don't,' I said.

'You do and you *do*,' he said.

I remembered when another doctor made the news. A young retarded boy had found his father's gun, and while the family slept, he shot them all in bed. The police asked the boy what he had done. But the boy went mute. He told them nothing. Then they called in the doctor.

'We know *you* didn't do it,' the doctor said to the boy, 'but tell me, did the *gun* do it?'

And yes, the boy was eager to tell him just what that gun had done.

I wanted the same out, and Dr Diamond wouldn't let me have it.

'Dr Diamond,' I said, 'I am giving up.'

'Now you are ready to begin,' he said.

I thought of Andean alpaca because that was what I planned to work up next. The feel of that yarn was not the only wonder – there was also the name of it: Alpaquita Superfina.

Dr Diamond was right.

I was ready to begin.

Beg, sl tog, inc, cont, rep.

Begin, slip together, increase, continue, repeat.

Dr Diamond answered the door. He said Dale Anne had run to the store. He was leaving, too, flying to a conference back East. The baby was asleep, he said, I should make myself at home.

I left my bag of knitting in the hall and went into Dale Anne's kitchen. It had been a year. I could have looked in on the baby. Instead, I washed the dishes that were soaking in the sink. The scouring pad was steel wool waiting for knitting needles.

The kitchen was filled with specialized utensils. When Dale Anne couldn't sleep she watched TV, and that's where the stuff was advertised. She had a thing to core tomatoes – it was called a Tomato Shark – and a metal spaghetti wheel for measuring out spaghetti. She had plastic melon-ballers and a push-in device that turned ordinary cake into ladyfingers.

I found pasta primavera in the refrigerator. My fingers wanted to knit the cold linguini, laying precisely cabled strands across the oily red peppers and beans.

Dale Anne opened the door.

'*Look* out, gal,' she said, and dropped a shopping bag on the counter.

I watched her unload ice-cream, potato chips, carbonated drinks and cake.

'It's been a long time since I walked into a market and expressed myself,' she said.

She turned to toss me a carton of cigarettes.

'Wait for me in the bedroom,' she said. '*West Side Story* is on.'

I went in and looked at the colour set. I heard the blender crushing ice in the kitchen. I adjusted the contrast, then Dale Anne handed me an enormous peach daiquiri. The goddamn thing had a tide factor.

Dale Anne left the room long enough to bring in the take-out chicken. She upended the bag on a plate and picked out a leg and a wing.

'I like my dinner in a bag and my life in a box,' she said, nodding towards the TV.

We watched the end of the movie, then part of a lame detective programme. Dale Anne said the show *owed* Nielsen four points, and reached for the *TV Guide*.

'Eleven-thirty,' she read. '*The Texas Whiplash Massacre*: Un-expected stop signs were their weapon.'

'Give me that,' I said.

Dale Anne said there was supposed to be a comet. She said we could probably see it if we watched from the living room. Just to be sure, we pushed the couch up close to the window. With the lights off, we could see everything without it seeing us. Although both of us had quit, we smoked at either end of the couch.

'Save my place,' Dale Anne said.

She had the baby in her arms when she came back in. I looked at the sleeping child and thought, Mercy, Land Sakes, Lordy Me. As though I had aged fifty years. For just a moment then I wanted nothing that I had and everything I did not.

'He told his first joke today,' Dale Anne said.

'What do you mean he told a joke?' I said. 'I didn't think they could talk.'

'Well, he didn't really *tell* a joke – he poured his orange juice over his head, and when I started after him, he said, "Raining?"'

'"Raining?" That's what he said? The kid is a genius,' I told Dale Anne. 'What Art Linkletter could do with this kid.'

Dale Anne laid him down in the middle of the couch, and we watched him or watched the sky.

'What a gyp,' Dale Anne said at dawn.

There had not been a comet. But I did not feel cheated, or even tired. She walked me to the door.

The knitting bag was still in the hall.

'Open it later,' I said. 'It's a sweater for him.'

But Dale Anne had to see it then.

She said the blue one matched his eyes and the camel one matched his hair. The red would make him glow, she said, and then she said, 'Help me out.'

Cables had become too easy; three more sweaters had pic-tures knitted in. They buttoned up the front. Dale Anne held up a parade of yellow ducks.

There were the Fair Isles, too – one in the pattern called Tree of Life, another in the pattern called Hearts.

It was an excess of sweaters – a kind of precaution, a rehearsal against disaster.

Dale Anne looked at the two sweaters still in the bag. 'Are you really OK?' she said.

The worst of it is over now, and I can't say that I am glad. Lose that sense of loss – you have gone and lost something else. But the body moves towards health. The mind, too, in steps. One step at a time. Ask a mother who has just lost a child, How many children do you have? 'Four,' she will say, '– three,' and years later, 'Three,' she will say, '– four.'

It's the little steps that help. Weather, breakfast, crossing with the light – sometimes it is all the pleasure I can bear to sleep, and know that on a rack in the bath, damp wool is pinned to dry.

Dale Anne thinks she would like to learn to knit. She measures the baby's crib and I take her over to Ingrid's. Ingrid steers her away from the baby pastels, even though they are machine-washable. Use a pure wool, Ingrid says. Use wool in a grown-up shade. And don't boast of your achievements or you'll be making things for the neighbourhood.

On Fair Isle there are only five women left who knit. There is not enough lichen left growing on the island for them to dye their yarn. But knitting machines can't produce their designs, and they keep on, these women, working the undyed colours of the sheep.

I wait for Dale Anne in the room with the patterns. The songs in these books are like lullabies to me.

K tog rem st. Knit together remaining stitches.

Cast off loosely.

The Youngest Doll

ROSARIO FERRÉ

Early in the morning the maiden aunt took her rocking chair out on to the porch facing the cane fields, as she always did whenever she woke up with the urge to make a doll. As a young woman, she had often bathed in the river, but one day when the heavy rains had fed the dragontail current, she had a soft feeling of melting snow in the marrow of her bones. With her head nestled among the black rocks' reverberations, she could hear the slamming of salty foam on the beach rolled up with the sound of waves, and she suddenly thought that her hair had poured out to sea at last. At that very moment, she felt a sharp bite in her calf. Screaming, she was pulled out of the water and, writhing in pain, was taken home on a stretcher.

The doctor who examined her assured her it was nothing, that she had probably been bitten by an angry river prawn. But days passed and the scab wouldn't heal. A month later the doctor concluded that the prawn had worked its way into the soft flesh of her calf and had nestled there to grow. He prescribed a mustard plaster so that the heat would force it out. The aunt spent a whole week with her leg covered with mustard from thigh to ankle, but when the treatment was over, they found that the ulcer had grown even larger and that it was covered with a slimy, stone-like substance that couldn't be removed without endangering the whole leg. She then resigned herself to living with the prawn permanently curled up in her calf.

She had been very beautiful, but the prawn hidden under the long, gauzy folds of her skirt stripped her of all vanity. She locked herself up in her house, refusing to see any suitors. At first she devoted herself entirely to bringing up her sister's children, dragging her enormous leg around the house quite nimbly. In those days, the family was nearly ruined; they lived surrounded by a past that was breaking up around them with the same impassive musicality with which the dining-room chandelier crumbled on the frayed linen cloth of the dining-room table. Her nieces adored her. She would comb their hair, bathe and feed them, and when she read them stories, they would sit around her and furtively lift the starched ruffle of her skirt so as to sniff the aroma of ripe sweetsop that oozed from her leg when it was at rest.

As the girls grew up, the aunt devoted herself to making dolls for them to play with. At first they were just plain dolls, with cotton stuffing from the gourd tree and stray buttons sewn on for eyes. As time passed, though, she began to refine her craft, gaining the respect and admiration of the whole family. The birth of a doll was always cause for a ritual celebration, which explains why it never occurred to the aunt to sell them for profit, even when the girls had grown up and the family was beginning to fall into need. The aunt had continued to increase the size of the dolls so that their height and other measurements conformed to those of each of the girls. There were nine of them, and the aunt made one doll for each per year, so it became necessary to set aside a room for the dolls alone. When the eldest turned eighteen there were one hundred and twenty-six dolls of all ages in the room. Opening the door gave the impression of entering a dovecot, or the ballroom in the Tsarina's palace, or a warehouse in which someone had spread out a row of tobacco leaves to dry. But the aunt did not enter the room for any of these pleasures. Instead, she would unlatch the door and gently pick up each doll, murmuring a lullaby as she rocked it: 'This is how you were when you were a year old, this is you at two, and like this at three,' measuring out each year of their lives against the hollow they left in her arms.

The day the eldest had turned ten, the aunt sat down in her rocking chair facing the cane fields and never got up again. She would rock away entire days on the porch, watching the patterns of rain shift in the cane fields, coming out of her stupor only when the doctor paid a visit or whenever she awoke with the desire to make a doll. Then she would call out so that everyone in the house would come and help her. On that day, one could see the hired help making repeated trips to town like cheerful Inca messengers, bringing wax, porcelain clay, lace, needles, spools of thread of every colour. While these preparations were taking place, the aunt would call the niece she had dreamt about the night before into her room and take her measurements. Then she would make a wax mask of the child's face, covering it with plaster on both sides, like a living face wrapped in two dead ones. She would draw out an endless flaxen thread of melted wax through a pin-point on its chin. The porcelain of the hands and face was always translucent; it had an ivory tint to it that formed a great contrast with the curled whiteness of the bisque faces. For the body, the aunt would send out to the garden for twenty glossy gourds. She would hold them in one hand, and with an expert twist of her knife, would slice them up against the railing of the balcony, so that the sun and breeze would dry out the cottony *guano* brains. After a few days, she would scrape off the dried fluff with a teaspoon and, with infinite patience, feed it into the doll's mouth.

The only items the aunt would agree to use that were not made by her were the glass eyeballs. They were mailed to her from Europe in all colours, but the aunt considered them useless until she had left them submerged at the bottom of the stream for a few days, so that they could learn to recognize the slightest stirring of the prawns' antennae. Only then would she carefully rinse them in ammonia water and place them, glossy as gems and nestled in a bed of cotton, at the bottom of one of her Dutch cookie tins. The dolls were always dressed in the same way, even though the girls were growing up. She would dress the younger ones in Swiss embroidery and the older ones in silk *guipure*, and on each of their heads she would tie the same bow, wide and white and trembling like the breast of a dove.

The girls began to marry and leave home. On their wedding day, the aunt would give each of them their last doll, kissing them on the forehead and telling them with a smile, 'Here is your Easter Sunday.' She would reassure the grooms by explaining to them that the doll was merely a sentimental ornament, of the kind that people used to place on the lid of grand pianos in the old days. From the porch, the aunt would watch the girls walk down the staircase for the last time. They would carry a modest checkered cardboard suitcase in one hand, the other hand slipped around the waist of the exuberant doll made in their image and likeness, still wearing the same old-fashioned kid slippers and gloves, and with Valenciennes bloomers barely showing under their snowy, embroidered skirts. But the hands and faces of these new dolls looked less transparent than those of the old: they had the consistency of skimmed milk. This difference concealed a more subtle one: the wedding doll was never stuffed with cotton but filled with honey.

All the older girls had married and only the youngest was left at home when the doctor paid his monthly visit to the aunt, bringing along his son who had just returned from studying medicine up north. The young man lifted the starched ruffle of the aunt's skirt and looked intently at the huge, swollen ulcer which oozed a perfumed sperm from the tip of its greenish scales. He pulled out his stethoscope and listened to her carefully. The aunt thought he was listening for the breathing of the prawn to see if it was still alive, and she fondly lifted his hand and placed it on the spot where he could feel the constant movement of the creature's antennae. The young man released the ruffle and looked fixedly at his father. 'You could have cured this from the start,' he told him. 'That's true,' his father answered, 'but I just wanted you to come and see the prawn that has been paying for your education these twenty years.'

From then on it was the young doctor who visited the old aunt every month. His interest in the youngest was evident from the start, so the aunt was able to begin her last doll in plenty of time.

He would always show up wearing a pair of brightly polished shoes, a starched collar, and an ostentatious tie-pin of extravagantly poor taste. After examining the aunt, he would sit in the parlour, lean his paper silhouette against the oval frame of the chair and, each time, hand the youngest an identical bouquet of purple forget-me-nots. She would offer him ginger cookies, taking the bouquet squeamishly with the tips of her fingers as if she were handling a sea urchin turned inside out. She made up her mind to marry him because she was intrigued by his sleepy profile and also because she was deathly curious to see what the dolphin flesh was like.

On her wedding day, as she was about to leave the house, the youngest was surprised to find that the doll her aunt had given her as a wedding present was warm. As she slipped her arm around its waist, she looked at it curiously, but she quickly forgot about it, so amazed was she at the excellence of its craft. The doll's face and hands were made of the most delicate Mikado porcelain. In the doll's half-open and slightly sad smile, she recognized her full set of baby teeth. There was also another notable detail: the aunt had embedded her diamond eardrops inside the doll's pupils.

The young doctor took her off to live in town, in a square house that made one think of a cement block. Each day he made her sit out on the balcony, so that passers-by would be sure to see that he had married into high society. Motionless inside her cubicle of heat, the youngest began to suspect that it wasn't only her husband's silhouette that was made of paper, but his soul as well. Her suspicions were soon confirmed. One day, he pried out the doll's eyes with the tip of his scalpel and pawned them for a fancy gold pocket watch with a long embossed chain. From then on the doll remained seated on the lid of the grand piano, but with her gaze modestly lowered.

A few months later, the doctor noticed the doll was missing from her usual place and asked the youngest what she'd done with it. A sisterhood of pious ladies had offered him a healthy sum for the porcelain hands and face, which they thought would be perfect for the image of the Veronica in the next Lenten procession.

The youngest answered that the ants had at last discovered the doll was filled with honey and, streaming over the piano, had devoured it in a single night. 'Since its hands and face were of Mikado porcelain,' she said, 'they must have thought they were made of sugar and at this very moment they are most likely wearing down their teeth, gnawing furiously at its fingers and eyelids in some underground burrow.' That night the doctor dug up all the ground around the house, to no avail.

As the years passed, the doctor became a millionaire. He had slowly acquired the whole town as his clientele, people who didn't mind paying exorbitant fees in order to see a genuine member of the extinct sugar cane aristocracy up close. The youngest went on sitting in her rocking chair on the balcony, motionless in her muslin and lace, and always with lowered eyelids. Whenever her husband's patients, draped with neck-laces and feathers and carrying elaborate canes, would seat themselves beside her, shaking their self-satisfied rolls of flesh with a jingling of coins, they would notice a strange scent that would involuntarily remind them of a slowly oozing sweetsop. They would then feel an uncomfortable urge to rub their hands together as though they were paws.

There was only one thing missing from the doctor's otherwise perfect happiness. He noticed that although he was ageing, the youngest still kept that same firm porcelained skin she had had when he would call on her at the big house on the plantation. One night he decided to go into her bedroom to watch her as she slept. He noticed that her chest wasn't moving. He gently placed his stethoscope over her heart and heard a distant swish of water. Then the doll lifted her eyelids, and out of the empty sockets of her eyes came the frenzied antennae of all those prawns.

The Ripening of Time

GAIL CHESTER

Motti and Shaindl had been friends for ever – at least since they were in Miss Grossman's class at kindergarten. Motti's parents lived at the better end of Hendon; his father had done rather well in business and was high up in the shul. Shaindl's parents, though greatly respected in the community, lived in a more modest house some ten minutes walkaway. Her mother kept complaining, until Shaindl was sick of hearing it, that she was always the one to help the children across the busy roads when they played at each other's house, never Motti's mother. Motti's mother knew nothing of this resentment and thought what a kind soul Mrs Levy was to put herself out for the kinnder. Shaindl had a resentment of her own – she thought that Motti and herself were quite capable of crossing any road in Hendon long before her mother did, so she couldn't see what all the fuss was about. Motti just shrugged when she complained to him, as if mothers were acts of God, way beyond his control.

As Shaindl and Motti grew older, their parents waited for them to grow out of their friendship. Motti's mother even mentioned it to Shaindl's, tactfully, so that she wouldn't take offence – God forbid that she should think for a moment that I am suggesting Shaindl isn't good enough for our boy, as she said to her husband. Motti's father was perplexed. 'What are you talking about, dear, they are only twelve, Motti isn't barmitzvah yet.'

'I was betrothed at their age,' she replied.

'But people don't get betrothed so young these days. I don't intend to arrange it. Do you?'

'No . . . but people will start to talk.'

'Let them . . .'

'It's all very well for you to say that. You don't have to go into the butcher's or sit under a hairdrier after the mikveh, or collect the children from school.'

'What's so terrible about two twelve-year-olds being friends?' he persisted.

'You're a dreamer, Joe, haven't you noticed she's a girl and he's a boy?'

'You mean Shaindl has been complaining to you as well about not having a barmitzvah?' Motti's mother was not amused.

Neither was Shaindl's, when she was telling her husband about the conversation with Mrs Rosen. '. . . Then she as good as said our Shaindl wasn't good enough for Motti.'

'I'm sure she would never say such a thing. They treat Shaindl as one of the family.'

'Yes, the poor relation.'

'I've been thinking myself lately that it's not right for a boy and girl their age to spend so much time together,' Mr Levy went on.

'I thought you were pleased that Shaindl was taking so much interest in Motti's barmitzvah portion – she says she knows it better than he does.'

'It's not healthy, a girl taking so much interest in studying, not a barmitzvah portion anyway.'

'You think we should stop her seeing him so much?'

'You're her mother, you know what's best.'

'It's a pity Shaindl doesn't recognize that too. What did we do to deserve such a headstrong daughter?'

Mr Levy shrugged.

Motti's barmitzvah was a triumph. Motti read so well in shul, the rabbi gave such a complimentary sermon, the party was so splendid. Everybody said so, even Mrs Levy. She bought Shaindl a dress for the occasion – small compensation for not having the actual barmitzvah. Of course, she had to spoil it by saying just before they left for the party, 'You know, Shaindl, you look so pretty when you make the effort. Why can't you do it more often?'

Shaindl stalked off to the car without replying. She decided that in future she would wear nothing but sacks tied round the middle with string. When they arrived at the reception, Motti, who she was sure wouldn't notice the difference between such an outfit and the most elegant ball-gown, greeted her with a wolf-whistle. She blushed scarlet and for the first time in her life didn't know what to say to him. Instead, she aimed a kick at his shins, but he laughed and moved out of her way saying, 'Now don't mess up my barmitzvah suit. Remember I've got to make a speech in it – the eyes of the world will be on me.'

'Yeah, and who wrote most of your speech?'

'Sorry. I guess I'm nervous. Thanks for your help. Now there's Aunt Millie and Uncle Reuben. I'll have to go and be polite.'

As soon as the barmitzvah was over, Motti got the flu. Shaindl phoned to ask after the invalid. 'Too much excitement,' said his father, 'the same thing happened to me. So how are you?'

'Bored,' said Shaindl. 'Can't I come round to see him?'

'Not for a few days. You know, I really think it's time you two found something else to do apart from sitting around at home on a Shabbos afternoon. What about joining Rimmon?'

'Ugh, I'm not spending my time with that bunch of snobs. All they do is sit around being horrible about people and talking about clothes.'

'You surprise me. I've known Stephen, the group leader, since he was a little schnip. I never suspected he spent his spare time discussing the latest fashions.'

Shaindl laughed heartily at the idea of such a serious young man doing anything so frivolous. But she knew what she was talking about. It was all very well during the formal part of the meeting. You sang a few songs, played a few games, studied a bit from that week's sidra. You might even get a piece of cake to go with the orange squash if you were lucky. It was afterwards that worried Shaindl, that agonizing hour before you could go home without seeming rude, when you had to talk to people, be sociable. At school her friends were either not frum or not Jewish – them she could talk to, though, of course, only at school. At home she had Motti. She sometimes wondered how he got on at his school.

'I've been thinking,' he said, when he had recovered from the flu, 'maybe it would be worth giving Rimmon a go.'

'Your parents have been getting at you,' she said accusingly. He didn't reply.

'You'll do anything for a quiet life, won't you?'

'I just thought it was worth trying. If we don't like it we can stop going.'

'I can tell you now that we won't like it. Well, you may like it, but I already know what it's like. I hear the girls talking at kosher dinners.'

They started going anyway. It did make Saturday afternoons pass faster, it did keep their parents quiet and some of the others were not so bad. But Shaindl resented the way the boys and girls were separated a lot of the time – not that she wanted to talk to the boys, she couldn't imagine what some of the girls saw in them – but she didn't like being restricted.

Walking home one week with Motti, she was shocked when he told her that some of the boys who went to non-Jewish schools took their tzitzis off on gym days, and one or two didn't wear them at all. She could understand their embarrassment – one reason she was glad not to be a boy was that she didn't have the tzitzis problem and she didn't have the hat problem. Wearing an extra vest with long fringes at the corners must take some explaining in the changing room. Motti said he thought that was one of the reasons his parents had insisted he went to a Jewish school – to spare him shame. But Shaindl couldn't imagine Motti being ashamed anywhere. He wasn't like those boys who swaggered along the road after Rimmon meetings, their trilbies at a rakish angle, like they were auditioning for bit parts in a gangster movie. She supposed they did it to try and prove they didn't feel conspicuous, but all they achieved was to look like orthodox Jewish boys whose hats weren't on straight.

Of course it was just as easy to pick out the frum girls, parading in groups every Shabbos afternoon, their clothes and hair just a bit neater, their hems and sleeves just a bit longer. Never exactly unfashionable, but never fashionable either. Shaindl had no interest in clothes, nor money to indulge it, but once in a while she would fantasize about walking down Brent Street wearing some outrageous outfit and with lots of make-up. You might get away with trousers during the week but never on Shabbos. Make-up wasn't allowed on Shabbos either, and anyway it was, as her mother said, fast.

As they got a bit older, Shaindl noticed a hint of lipstick appearing on some of the girls' mouths, the merest suggestion of mascara on their lashes. These were the girls the boys went out with, even though they all knew that frum boys and girls did not go out with each other. Nevertheless, discreet hand-holding seemed to be leading to trips to the cinema when Shabbos went out early enough, and then the boys would remove their cappels in the back row of the stalls, as if God would not then notice them snogging in the dark. And what cappels the boys wore, Shaindl wondered why they bothered – the size of sixpenny pieces they were, they could easily get lost in the hair on the top of their heads. The hypocrisy of it all was getting to her. She began to ask Motti again why they kept going to Rimmon week after week. 'It's not as if we participate in the main activity that goes on there these days,' she said.

'What's that?'

'You mean you haven't noticed?'

'I mean, I don't think it has changed much.'

'Well, you and I may not have changed much, but as far as the others are concerned, going to Rimmon is about having boy-friends and girlfriends in a way our parents can handle.'

'So why are we missing out?'

'I suppose everyone thinks we are going out with each other already.'

84

'Do you?'

'Of course not.'

Motti looked incredibly relieved.

Shaindl thought a lot about that look of relief. She knew how she felt but it wasn't relief exactly, more a sense of security that she didn't have to compete where she knew she couldn't win. But Motti didn't have anything to worry about – he was tall and good-looking. He could go out with any of the girls he wanted. She had once overheard Stella Goldbloom say as much to someone in the toilets at school. The girls clearly thought Motti was out of his mind to hang around with Shaindl. Shaindl had been very upset at the time, though she hadn't said anything. Who could she say it to?

So, now they were in the sixth form, and having to think about the future, which as far as their parents were concerned did not require all that much thought. Motti would go to yeshiva at Gateshead for a year or two before going to London University to study law. Shaindl was a clever girl, so she would go to university too, in London of course. It didn't seem to matter too much what she studied. Then she and Motti would get married when their studies were finished. Motti seemed quite content with this arrangement – Shaindl was not.

'If I don't get away from home soon I'll go mad,' she told Motti one evening when they met for a rare walk after their homework. Motti looked mildly surprised at this idea.

'It's all right for you,' Shaindl went on, 'you're going away anyway.'

'I'm just going to yeshiva to study, with lots of other boys like me, only maybe from Leeds, instead of London. It's not exactly escape into travel and adventure.'

'Better than staying here. Take me with you. Please, take me with you.'

'How can I do that? I'm going to yeshiva. I want to study before starting my law degree. Anyway, you'll be at university.'

'We could get married now. Durham or Newcastle are close to Gateshead, you could study and I could go to university there.

We wouldn't get in each other's way at all. Oh, please, Motti, otherwise I'll be stuck here for ever.'

For the first time in their long friendship, in all the years of Shaindl's bold ideas, Motti shouted at her. 'What do you take me for?' he roared. 'I'm not some sort of lapdog to bend to your will. You haven't even asked me how I feel about getting married. What sort of meshugana idea is this?'

Shaindl was so surprised she burst into tears.

'I thought you were my best friend. Friends help each other out. I thought . . .'

'That's just it, you didn't think.'

'You're right, I didn't think, but I'm thinking now. I think you are more interested in the boys at yeshiva than you are in helping your best friend. Otherwise why would you be behaving like this?'

Motti seemed genuinely puzzled. 'What do you mean?'

Shaindl stopped crying and looked at Motti as though she was seeing him for the first time. Slowly and carefully, she went on, 'I didn't understand what I meant either, until a moment ago. Now I understand why we have been such good friends for all these years. I was your protection and you were mine.'

'Protection? Against what?'

'If you don't see it, my dearest friend, I can't explain it. But go home and think about it, and then tell me why we shouldn't get married now. I think it makes the best sense in the world, it could be the only way out for both of us. You get your yeshiva and I get my liberty.'

The next day, Shaindl was passing the end of Motti's street on the way home from school. She had no intention of calling in, as she sometimes did; she might ring later. Suddenly her sleeve was tugged very hard from behind, and she heard Motti's mother say,

'Just a moment, young lady, I want a word with you.'

'Oh, hello, Mrs Rosen. You made me jump.'

'I'll do more than make you jump in a minute, my girl.'

'Pardon? Excuse me, Mrs Rosen, but would you mind telling me what is going on?'

'You don't know?'

'I haven't a clue.'

'But Motti said it was because of you.'

'It was because of me, what, Mrs Rosen?'

Motti's mother began to feel a bit foolish. Perhaps she had been jumping to conclusions? She let go of Shaindl's sleeve which she had been clutching insistently until then.

'Last night, Motti came back from his walk with you and said that you had made him see it was quite impossible for him to go to Gateshead, so now he needs time to rethink his future. So naturally, I assumed you had been influencing him with your meshugasim and trying to persuade him to abandon his studies.'

Shaindl tried to calm her down. 'Quite the reverse, Mrs Rosen, I do assure you. I spent a long time telling him how much I thought he would benefit from the experience, and I even suggested that it might be possible – with your permission of course – for us to consider getting married now, so that I could be with him while he was studying.'

'Did you really?' Mrs Rosen was amazed. 'I think you had better come in for a cup of tea, and maybe we can sort this out.'

'No, I think it would be better if we left it for now. Poor Motti is obviously upset about something. It might be wiser to speak to him on the phone later.'

'Maybe you're right, my dear. Why don't you run along home and we'll all speak later, when Mr Rosen gets home.'

Shaindl carried on down the road, her brain spinning. Why had Motti suddenly decided against yeshiva? Why was he blaming her? She hoped Mrs Rosen hadn't phoned her mother. If she had there would be hell to pay when she got home. And then there was her UCCA form – the deadline for applying to university was so soon and she couldn't bear the thought of her father standing over her while she filled in five London places. She had been amazed when the form arrived to see that nowhere on it was she required to get her parents' signature – my first adult decision, she had thought with delight, until her father told her flatly that he would not pay his share of the grant if she went anywhere away from home. 'But I can't manage without your contribution,' she protested. Her father hadn't replied. And now Motti hated her as well. But what on earth was he going to do if he didn't go to Gateshead? He had been so angry with her last night – he would probably never speak to her again, and even if he did, any assistance from that direction was obviously out of the question now. How could she get through the next few months without his friendship, never mind being imprisoned at home after they left school? Maybe she should abandon university next year and get a job, then she could save up enough to go away from London the year after. But living with her parents for that year would be hell, and then when she left it would be for ever. No, that wouldn't do. Maybe she could go to Israel for a year, her parents would probably agree to that, then she could reconsider. But she didn't want to be forced out of the country. That was probably what Motti was planning to do, take the acceptable way out, she thought maliciously, leaving me stranded.

Almost as soon as she got home, the phone rang. It was Motti, sounding rather subdued.

'I was wondering whether you would be free this evening for a chat?' he inquired cautiously.

'I expect I can fit you in,' she tried to sound off-hand.

'Thing is, I don't want to talk to you at home. Could we meet in the park, or somewhere?'

'I should think so, but I don't know what time Mum's coming home, what to do about supper. She'll kick up if I'm not here.'

'Leave a note telling her it's a matter of life and death.'

'Is it?'

'Definitely.'

'OK then, I'll meet you by the duckpond in twenty minutes, and I'll even bring some stale bread to make it look convincing.'

Shaindl rapidly prepared some vegetables, scribbled a note and rushed out of the house before her mother could arrive to

detain her. She couldn't imagine explaining Motti's sudden
erratic behaviour, especially when everybody knew she was the
wild, unpredictable one. 'I bet he didn't have to stop and peel
potatoes,' she thought irritably as she turned the corner before
the pond. Catching sight of Motti, uncharacteristically slumped
on a bench, she could sense the misery in his motionless form. A
great surge of affection swept through her, taking her quite by
surprise. She slid quietly on to the bench beside him, linking her
arm through his and sat, swinging her legs and waiting for him to
speak.

After a long silence, he turned to her and said, 'You were
quite right – about the boys, I mean. I owe you an apology. You
forced me to recognize things . . . It isn't that I don't want to
marry you – I don't want to marry anyone. I think you're the
nicest girl in the whole world – in fact, the nicest person in the
whole world. But it isn't girls I'm interested in . . .'

'I know that,' murmured Shaindl.

'And once I realized that,' Motti continued, 'I realized it
would be dishonest for me to go to Gateshead. I would be going
for the wrong reasons and I have to face who I really am. I can't
take my parents' money and study, then come back and not
marry you. You made me see that.'

'So, what will you do instead?'

'I thought I'd go right away somewhere, where no one knows
me, and start again. Sort myself out.'

'And how will you do that? What will you do for money?'

'I don't know,' he confessed lamely.

'I can just picture the scene – nice Jewish boy from good
home, never done anything more strenuous than turn the page
of a textbook, never eaten a morsel of traife food, sets out into
the wide world to seek his fortune. Were you thinking of
becoming a navvy, or maybe joining the Foreign Legion?'

Motti looked so dejected, Shaindl had to laugh.

'What's so bloody funny?' he asked wearily.

Shaindl leaned across and for the first time ever, kissed him full
on the lips. This time he looked so startled, she laughed again.

'I don't understand,' he said, 'after what I just told you, how can you bear to kiss me?'

'Because you are my best friend and I love you, as my best friend,' said Shaindl tenderly. 'And I won't hear of you running away to sea – or even Israel, which is what I thought you might suggest – unless you take me with you.' She held her hand up to silence him as he opened his mouth to protest.

'Don't you understand by now that I'm offering us both the perfect escape? Nobody will ever guess; we'll both be happy, and our parents will give us their blessing.'

'But it wouldn't be right.'

'They'd be getting exactly what they want – one married yeshiva bochur, with a very desirable wife, if I may say so.'

Motti started to laugh. Shaindl sensed she was winning him round.

'Shall we go and tell your parents the good news first, or mine?'

'Not so fast, I haven't agreed yet.'

'But you will, won't you?'

He didn't demur as she pulled him to his feet and they set off back to his parents' house.

Ms Snow White Wins Case in High Court

CLODAGH CORCORAN

In a landmark decision handed down in Court yesterday by Ms Justice Goodbye, Snow White was granted an injunction against seven men. MARK MIWORD reports on the case.

Snow White was yesterday granted an injunction in the High Court in Dublin, restraining a total of seven men from entering on or interfering with the premises in the heart of the woods, which had been shared between them for ten years. The Court heard how Ms White had been abused for a total of ten years by the defendants, since she was seven years old. In an extempore judgement, Ms Justice Goodbye said that it was the worst case she had ever been forced to hear.

At the conclusion of the hearing, which lasted four days, there was uproar from the seven defendants, who had to be carried forcibly from the body of the Court. Gardai were forced to arrest three of the defendants as they emerged, and all pleaded guilty to a breach of the peace in a special sitting of the District Court, and were fined £2 each and bound over.

Yesterday was devoted entirely to the judgement, as evidence had been taken earlier from both the plaintiff and the defendants. In outlining the evidence which had been given, Justice Goodbye said that it was obvious that the defendants had, by their own admission, never made any attempt to offer retribution to Ms White, and that the worst aspect of the entire case was that they had shown no remorse for their actions over the years. In fact, the contrary was the case, as the defendants sought to justify their behaviour, and thereby compounded the wrong.

Justice Goodbye outlined the circumstances under which the case came before her. Ms White had been abandoned in the heart of the forest, when she was seven years old, by an agent acting on behalf of her stepmother, who wished to get rid of her. She pointed out, *inter alia*, that it was open to bring an action for cruelty on foot of this. Ms White, after wandering around for some considerable time, had then stumbled on a small house. Exhausted, she had lain down to sleep. Upon awakening, she was confronted by seven men, who were returning home from work as gold-diggers. Justice Goodbye made the point that Ms White was in no fit mental or physical condition, by virtue of her age and circumstances, to make any decision which could amount under any circumstances to mean 'the right to choose', in the legal sense of the word. Consequently, everything which took place following the initial encounter was tainted.

Messrs Dopey, Sneezy, Happy, Grumpy, Doc, Sleepy and Bashful proceeded to enter into a contract with Ms White, who was still exhausted, and in any event, of an age not legally held to be old enough to enter into a contract. Effectively under duress, Ms White agreed – following various promptings from the seven men – to look after the house while they were out gold-digging. She also agreed to cook and wash for all seven, to make all the beds, to sew and knit and generally look after their welfare. Ms Justice Goodbye said that the contract, apart from its earlier mentioned failings, was derelict further in so far as there was no limit to the contractual obligations entered upon by Ms White. In return for agreeing to those conditions, Ms White was allowed to sleep in the house, and also have enough food to eat. The contract was, in the words of Justice Goodbye, 'a travesty of natural justice'. She said also that Ms White must have been 'the handiest slave these seven men would ever have the good fortune to encounter.'

The seven men were so content with their lot that they took to singing songs upon their exit from the house each morning, and upon their return in the evening. Ms Justice Goodbye outlined the duties which Ms White was expected to perform. She was forced to get up two hours before any of the seven men, and prepare their breakfast. At the same time, she had to gather wood to light the fire and ensure that the house was clean by the time the seven decided it was time for them to get up. She herself did not get anything to eat until they left. On occasion, there was very little food left and she was forced to wait until dinner-time before she ate properly.

With regard to the washing of their clothes, Ms Goodbye rehearsed the evidence that had been given to the effect that the seven never took any care of themselves when they were out digging for gold. Knowing that they had someone at home to do 'all the dirty work', their behaviour was such as to suggest that they were deliberately creating work for Snow White. Ms White had given evidence of the filthy nature of all seven men. They left their clothes where they fell before they went to bed, and she was expected to cater to their smallest whim. This, said Justice Goodbye, was somewhat at odds with the claim of the defendants' Counsel that all seven were self-styled New Age Men in touch with their own feelings and emotions. Throughout all of this, the seven men continually reminded Snow White that on no account should she attempt to open the door during their absence. To this end, they warned her about all manner of dangers which she might face should she disobey them. Justice Goodbye pointed out that even though this 'warning' might well be grounded in a genuine concern for Ms White's 'welfare', the defendants had brought no evidence forward during the hearing to support their claim. The result of these 'warnings' was that Ms White lived in virtual isolation for many years, unaware that around the cottage a small township, Crumlin, had grown up.

As Ms White reached maturity, it appeared to her that the seven men became more 'friendly', in her own words, and she believed that they were viewing her in a different light from hitherto. Gradually, it became clear that some of the seven had designs on her. Justice Goodbye pointed out that it was left to Ms White herself to make clear that 'conjugal rights' had been no part of the original contract. The Justice took the view that this was 'outlandish behaviour' on the part of some of the seven, and that 'it was an extension of the contract which no right-thinking person' would agree with.

The defendants, said Ms Justice Goodbye, had given evidence to the effect that throughout their careers as gold-diggers, they had made what they described as 'a fair bit of money'. However, none of this wealth had ever found its way to Ms White, nor indeed had gone any way towards making her life in the house any easier. The Justice said that the only conclusion that could be drawn was that the seven had hidden their wealth, and that they had no intention, even at this late stage, of making any amends to Ms White. The Justice also pointed out that it was open to Ms White to enter a claim on the entire property in the woods, with a view to ensuring complete title to the entire estate. The Justice felt that 'any Court in the land would surely look most favourably on any such claim.' Consequently, Justice Goodbye said that she had no hesitation in making an order restraining all seven defendants from entering on or interfering with the house in the woods. Leave to appeal was refused.

After the disturbances, during which one of the defendants, Mr Grumpy, started to shout abuse at the Justice, Ms White appeared outside the Court with her close friend and supporter, Ms Rapunzel. Speaking to reporters, Ms White said that her life had been 'like a bad fairytale' for the past ten years.

Last night, a spokesperson for the Council for New Age Men, said that they wished Ms White 'all the best for the future' but that the judgement itself held 'grimm prospects' for other cases in that every person who thought they had a similar case as Ms White might now take an action, but that the action might fail, and thus 'hopes would be raised which might not be fulfilled'. The Council said that it was exploring the setting up of a Working Party to look at the implications of this case for all gold-diggers. At some time in the future they may, or may not, publish a report.

Biographical Notes

LEONORA BRITO writes: 'I am in my thirties, and live and work in Cardiff.'

GAIL CHESTER was born in 1951 and brought up in an orthodox Jewish family in London. She gave up religion, then joined the Women's Liberation Movement in 1970 and has been active in feminism and radical politics ever since. She sings with the Pre-Madonnas, a feminist choir, and works in publishing. She has written articles and edited non-fiction anthologies but is a recent convert to fiction – the story in this book is her first to be published.

CLODAGH CORCORAN was born and educated in Dublin. Once upon a time she had her own children's bookshop, and since returning to Ireland from Yorkshire, is again working with children's books. She has edited short story collections – *Discoveries* and *Baker's Dozen* and, currently, *The Ultimate Irish Children's Joke Book*. She founded the Mother Goose Award for children's book illustration. Most of the time she is happy.

ROSARIO FERRÉ was born in Puerto Rico. She has written children's stories, poems, feminist essays, a novel and literary criticism on fantastic literature. She believes the fantastic to be a very powerful expression of the collective subconscious and has a great respect for magical occurrences. 'The Youngest Doll' was her first story.

AMY HEMPEL was born in 1951 in Chicago. She moved to California, the setting of her stories, in her teens. She had what she called 'your basic nonlinear education' at four colleges before taking a fiction workshop at Columbia. She has said, 'I am really interested in resilience' – this is evident in her writing.

JEAN HOLKNER writes: 'I was born in Perth, Western Australia, so long ago I don't even remember it. As a teenager I was taller than everyone else, inclined to fat, and had the biggest feet in the country. In spite of it all, I eventually found someone willing to marry me and I now have a reasonably normal son and a teenage grand-daughter who is short and slim. Lucky girl!'

DOROTHY NIMMO. Born in Manchester, educated York and Cambridge, spent the 50s acting in London, the 60s having four children in Geneva, the 70s raising them in Peterborough and the 80s in North Yorkshire gardening, goatherding and trying to be a mother. Went to the USA to find a new direction, came back to be caretaker of Gloucester Friends' Meeting House and to write.

KATE PULLINGER was born in 1961 in Canada where she lived until she moved to London at the age of twenty. Since then she has written short stories (collected in *Tiny Lies*) as well as a novel, *When the Monster Dies*. In 1987–8 she was writer in residence at the Battersea Arts Centre, London.

RAVINDER RANDHAWA says of herself: 'The first seven years of my life were spent in India and the rest in England. I have always wanted to write. Since I know that Asian women aren't the passive and silent creatures that many people try to make them out to be, I write stories with them as protagonists, looking at life through their eyes, as well as writing stories that are fun and exciting. I'm now working on my second novel *Flicksaw*.'

JANE ROGERS writes: 'I was born in London in 1952, and moved every few years until I ended up in Lancashire in 1980. I have worked in housing, as an English teacher and in adult education, but am now writing full time. I have two young children.

'True Romance' was the first story I had published; since then there have been three novels – most recently, *The Ice is Singing* – and a play for Channel 4.'

MARGARET SUTHERLAND writes: 'Writing helps me understand myself – the stories are about problems or conflicts I may not realize I have. I write about what I see and know – when I lived in New Zealand I set my books there; now I've shifted, my next book will have an Australian setting. I am starting a novel, and this feels exciting, scary and free, like setting off to some strange country on an adventure.'

Acknowledgements

The author and publishers wish to thank the following for their kind permission to include copyright material in this book:

Sheba Publishers for '. . . But Not By Dirt . . .' by Leonora Brito from *Charting the Journey: Writings by Black and Third World Women*, edited by Shabnam Grewal, Jackie Kay, Liliane Landor, Gail Lewis and Pratibha Parmar, copyright © Leonora Brito, 1988; Gail Chester for her story 'The Ripening of Time', copyright © Gail Chester, 1990; Attic Press, Dublin for 'Ms Snow White Wins Case in High Court' by Clodagh Corcoran, which first appeared in *Sweeping Beauties*, published by Attic Press, copyright © Clodagh Corcoran, 1989; Spinster/Aunt Lute for 'The Youngest Doll' by Rosario Ferré, which first appeared in *Reclaiming Medusa: Short Stories by Contemporary Puerto Rican Women*, published by Spinster/Aunt Lute, copyright © Rosario Ferré; Alfred A. Knopf Inc. for 'Beg, Sl Tog, Inc, Cont, Rep' by Amy Hemple from *Reasons to Live*, published by Alfred A. Knopf Inc., copyright © Amy Hemple; The Women's Press and Penguin Books Australia for 'Fat Chance' by Jean Holkner from *Aunt Becky's Wedding and Other Traumas*, first published by Penguin Books Australia as 'Taking the Chook', copyright © Jean Holkner, 1987, and first published in Great Britain by The Women's Press, 1989; Dorothy Nimmo for her story 'The Healing' which first appeared in *First Fictions: Introduction 9*, published by Faber and Faber Ltd, copyright © Dorothy Nimmo; Jonathan Cape Ltd for 'In Montreal' by Kate Pullinger from *Tiny Lies*, published by Jonathan Cape Ltd, copyright © Kate Pullinger, 1988; Ravinder Randhawa for her story 'War of the Worlds', which first appeared in *Right of Way*, published by The Women's Press, copyright © Asian Women Writers' Workshop, 1988; Peter Fraser & Dunlop for 'True Romance', originally entitled 'The Real Thing', which first appeared in *Spare Rib* magazine, copyright © Jane Rogers, 1978; Margaret Sutherland for 'Codling-Moth' from *One Whale Singing and Other Stories from New Zealand*, first published by Oxford University Press, New Zealand, copyright © Margaret Sutherland.